marchesa Colombi

The Wane of an Ideal

A novel

marchesa Colombi

The Wane of an Ideal
A novel

ISBN/EAN: 9783337028190

Printed in Europe, USA, Canada, Australia, Japan

Cover: Foto ©Andreas Hilbeck / pixelio.de

More available books at **www.hansebooks.com**

THE
WANE OF AN IDEAL

A NOVEL

BY

LA MARCHESA COLOMBI

FROM THE ITALIAN

BY

CLARA BELL

REVISED AND CORRECTED IN THE UNITED STATES

NEW YORK
WILLIAM S. GOTTSBERGER, PUBLISHER
11 MURRAY STREET
1885

THE WANE OF AN IDEAL.

CHAPTER I.

THERE was not a soul in all Fontanetto and the neighborhood who did not know the "little doctor." For twenty years he had been known by that name, ever since he had come there as the parish doctor. He was then a young man of about thirty, gallant, gay, and the best of good company. To distinguish him from his predecessor, the new-comer was dubbed with the nickname of "*Dottorino*," in some sort as a pet name, he was such an engaging man, and the name had clung to him ever since, in spite of years and the changes in his person, which entered a crying protest against the diminutive.

When I first knew him he may have been fifty, tall, stout, and burly. His broad shoulders, thick neck, powerful build, and coarse rough hair, revealed a robust constitution; but a certain heaviness in his eyes, the flabbiness of his cheeks, the slowness of his speech with a hesitation as if he had a difficulty in grasping the thought he wished to utter, and a queer squeak in his voice, made him seem older than he really was. But for all this he was none the less popular, and the gentry of the vicinity were always glad to have the little doctor at their dinners and evening parties— only not by their bedside when they were ill.

The little doctor knew of but one method of treatment, namely: the purgative; and he prescribed it for every kind and form of disease. When he was sent for to see a sick person, before he set out, before he even asked his symptoms, he began by stating positively: "A good strong dose —that is what he wants!" He commonly mistook the cause for the effect and with regard to that effect he was pleased to be highly facetious; the doctor's jokes were known far and wide. As he went along he would stop at a tavern, call for drink, and then say to the host: "Put it down against me; I will pay you with a visit the next time you want a pill." And he would laugh, and

the host laughed too. He had not always legs
enough to carry him upstairs to see his patient;
but what was the good of looking at him ? He
could quite as well prescribe for him at the door. He
would ask the people of the house : " What is the
matter with him — fever ? Give him a purgative.
Headache ? delirious ? give him a rattling dose ;
that will cure him of his delirium. An overloaded
stomach — that is the whole secret."

More than once the parish board had talked of
remonstrating with the Dottorino. But then the
gentry made much of him, and it never was allowed ; and he himself, when it came to his ears,
exclaimed with his usual jollity :

" But what next ? The parish ought to thank
me — I help to fertilize their land. It is to me that
they owe the juicy artichokes, the gigantic cab-
bages, the asparagus as thick as a cudgel that they
see on their tables. . . ."

It was impossible to get this great baby to be
serious about anything. He laughed with you over
your aches and pains, bringing out jest upon jest,
till you ended by opening a bottle to the health of
the little doctor whose joviality put you in such
good spirits. Besides, in case of grave illness, the

more important folks who had horses at their
command, could fetch the doctor in an hour from
Borgomanero; and the little doctor, being a
superior man, owed him no grudge. He let his
patients recover under any one in whom they believed when they were ill, without declining on
that account to eat and drink with them when
they got well again.

Whatever the time of day, or wherever he might
be, the doctor always dressed in black ; indeed, in
an old suit of dress clothes, much too short and
too tight. He wore an enormous white handkerchief folded into a cravat which went two or three
times around his throat, while the ends, tied into a
tight knot, made a lump on his neck, so that the
whole looked like a small goitre, When the Dottorino laughed this knot bobbed up and down, as
if it were some portion of his person, and shared
in his hilarity; when he drank it rose and fell with
a calm chuckle, as it were, of beatitude, as
though it knew good wine when it tasted it ; and
when the doctor was drunk and his whole person
became limp and unsteady, that knot, too, oscil-
lated with a languid and piteous air. On the top
of this ceremonial costume he wore a chimney-

pot hat, too wide in the brim and too low in the crown, and always a little cocked over the left ear. From the first day when the little doctor set foot in Fontanetto no one could remember ever having seen him in any other dress. He had married and had a son; then he was left a widower; and he had appeared in the same clothes at the wedding, at the christening, and at the funeral. For twenty years he had walked over hill and dale, by night and by day to the houses of the peasants who needed his services, and always in black dress clothes with a tall hat; it was as though he had been born in them and it was certain that he would die in them. If the little doctor had altered his mode of dress it would have been like a revolution in the little township.

CHAPTER II.

THE doctor had remained unmarried — with his one boy. "A widower has his own value in the market," he used to say, "but with a baby on his hands he is an unsaleable article. A man by himself is worth a good dowry, but a man and a half is worth nothing."

At first he left the child in care of the woman who had wet-nursed it; it could remain with her for a few years. At last, however, when the boy was six, he was forced to take him home; and can you not imagine the trouble he had with him.

He was a little wildling, an untamed little savage. No sooner had he got home than he cried the whole of one day for his nurse, screaming as loud as he could for his "mamma — I want my mamma." The Dottorino, hapless man, was not a woman, that he could stay coaxing a baby; he locked him up in one of the rooms and went about his business. When he returned in the evening all the neighborhood had gathered round the house with their noses pointing up to the windows. The child had been screaming for some hours, and the stairs were crowded with women who were pitying it and discussing what was to be done. The doctor had been drinking with his patients' sick-nurses; he was coming home in the best of humors. You may fancy what his feelings were at hearing those howls and at seeing these inquisitive good folks putting their noses into his private concerns. But he was not the man to make a scene; he pointed to the street-door as he addressed the gossips:

"I am the master here, perhaps you know," he said. "I will undertake to manage my own child and no one need interfere. If you do not know what parental authority is — go and learn. Now then, be off, in less than no time! Brrrrr!"

When he had gone in and shut the door upon them the child began to yell more loudly than ever; his cries were shrieks of pain, and so desperately piercing that they were heard from one end of the village to the other. By degrees they died away, and at last ceased altogether. Then the Dottorino came out, very red in the face, and his hands and his voice shook as he said to two obstinate old women whom he had not been able to turn out:

"Go and see if you can bring him round, and find me a girl to mind him or else. . . ."

Next morning all the gossips of the village came in procession to the doctor's house to offer him nursery girls. He had by this time recovered his temper.

"Give me," he said, "the youngest and best looking."

He was a man of taste and appreciated beauty, even of a rustic order. But the first damsel did not value the doctor's attentions and at the end of a few days she left. Then he found some who were more tractable and who stayed — nay, who would very gladly never have left, but those he himself dismissed. He had no intention of marrying again or adding to his responsibilities.

He had learnt by experience that there is no more thankless task than that of bringing up a family. The one child he had was an ungrateful little rascal. If he only heard his father's step he would begin to tremble and try to hide. If the doctor spoke he would start as if a pistol had been fired off close to his car, and always answered in monosyllables, while the servant girls would chat and laugh at his jokes.

Still the maids were constantly changing; the luckless doctor was at his wits' end to get a servant who would stay. On one occasion he was two months without a woman in the house, and he had to send the boy to school every day to get him out of the way.

But "Heaven helps the light-hearted," says an Italian proverb. One day he was sent for to see a young girl who was ill. He found her sitting in the sun, outside the kitchen door, and trembling with fever. He ordered her the usual purgative and then he asked the old woman who was standing by her side:

"Is she your daughter?"

"No, sir," replied old Lucia; "she came to us from the foundling hospital at Novara. My daughter-in-law lost all her babies; so when the last one was born she thought she would get a child to nurse; and then from day to day she put off taking her back again, and she ended by keeping her altogether. When they would not pay us any longer for keeping her we sent her to the silk mills, so that she might earn something. She has been at it now for six years, tying the silk ; she began early."

" And do you like working at the silk mills ?" the doctor asked the sick girl.

Her only reply was a wriggle of her whole body ; whether it was meant for an answer or was a more violent shiver it was impossible to decide.

" She talks very little," said the old woman, who, on the contrary, talked a great deal. "It is from having her head full of the whizzing and whirling of all those bobbins and spindles every day. It makes you feel stupid. I know, for I tried it for two years when I was a girl ; I always had a roaring in my ears as if it was pouring in torrents, and night and day I saw the spokes of the wheels flying round and round before my eyes, like souls in torment."

" How much a day does she get ?" asked the doctor.

" Twenty centimes. She is only thirteen."

" Twenty centimes a day, exclusive of Sundays and the regular holidays ; that is sixty francs a year," said the doctor making a rapid calculation. " If you will let her come to me for the same money I will take her to do the odd jobs in my house, and to mind my little boy. The work will not break her bones."

" But she does not know how to cook," observed Lucia.

" You will teach her what you can while she is ill, and as soon as she is well you can bring her to me."

" Well—yes," said the old woman, still doubtful. " But at the mills they will raise her wages when she is grown up."

" She is not strong enough to go on working at the mills; you will always have her at home ill, and so she will earn nothing," replied the Dottorino, rising to go.

But this last argument had convinced Lucia; she turned to the girl and said :

" Well, would you like to go and be the Signor Dottore's servant ? Answer, La Matta, would you ?"

The girl only shrugged her shoulders, as much as to say she did not care.

CHAPTER III.

A MONTH after this Lucia brought the young girl to the doctor's house in her holiday dress, her shoes in her hand and her feet bare, with all her little belongings tied up in a handkerchief knotted at the corners, and installed her under her new master.

In her remote youth Lucia had herself been in service with a family at Novara and she had learnt enough of cooking and management to put the girl in the way of discharging her duties. Her pupil, to be sure, stultified by the six long years she had passed in the midst of the confusion and din of the mills, always stood with her mouth open after listening to her instructions as if she had not understood ; but when once she had fairly learnt a thing she could repeat it to all eternity with the minutest exactitude, exactly like a machine. She brought the same painful attention that she had been forced to give to her work at the silk mill to bear on every little task — the unremitting watchfulness which was required to join the threads, keeping one eye as it were on the spool and the other on the spindle, catching the thread if it broke with nimble fingers, a quick eye and strained absorption of mind — a tension of fibre and nerve beyond her years. When once she had been taught to dust the legs of a table from the right hand to the left, no change of conditions could ever have led her to do it in the opposite direction, or to leave one of the legs untouched. When the doctor beat her—for he even had his ugly moods and felt that he must have it out with some one — La Matta crouched under his hand, and howled if she was hurt; but she made no complaint and never asked why she was punished so; on the other hand if her master praised her cookery and said : " You did that very well," she would shrug her shoulders as much as to say it was no concern of hers ; or reply : " I did not know it."

When as a new-born babe she had found her miserable home in the foundling hospital, her first protectress was a sentimental nun who had bestowed on her the inappropriate name of Amata. The peasant woman who had taken her out to

nurse, and all the family, had simplified this to La
Matta — the idiot — and in spite of the remonstrances of the good Sister and afterwards of
the inspector at the mills, they had persisted in
their blunder with the obstinacy that is character-
istic of peasants, so that all the neighborhood believed it really to be her name. One day Giovanni, the doctor's little lad, asked her:

" Why do they call you *La Matta !*"

" I do not know," said the girl.

" Is it your name ?"

" No. My name is La Mata."

" But Mata is not a name."

" I do not know."

Giovanni succeeded in arriving at some explanation from a school-fellow or from the Sister
who taught the village children, and on his return
home he went into the kitchen to repeat it in
triumph to the girl. But she only said:

" It is all the same ; La Mata or La Matta."

" But it is not La Mata at all; your name is
Amata ; L'Amata is right."

" Ah well ! I do not know," was La Matta's
conclusion, but she looked at the little fellow

with a long pathetic gaze and then smiled to herself.

One day on his return from school Giovanni found her with her face and eyes swelled with crying and the streaks left by tears on her cheeks.

" What is the matter ?" he asked. She put her hand to her left shoulder, writhing to show that it was painful.

" You have hurt yourself?" he said.

" Yes," nodded La Matta.

" Did you tumble down ?"

" No, it was when he was beating me — he pulled my arm."

" Who ?"

" He," she replied in a low voice, as though afraid that the doctor would hear her. She never called him anything but *he*.

" You are crying because he beat you ?"

" No, it is the pain that I am crying for." But at this catechism, which showed that some one cared for her, she smiled through her tears. That evening before putting the child to bed she said :

" Look here," and unfastening the body of her dress she uncovered her child's bosom and shoulder which was terribly swelled and black with bruises. The two looked at each other in dismay.

"What ought to be done to it?" asked Giovanni.

"I do not know." And then they looked at each other again. Presently Giovanni had an idea.

"I will ask the school-mistress to-morrow morning," he said. The girl smiled gratefully, covered up her innocent nudity and took her bruises to bed.

By the next morning the swelling had greatly increased; the arm was too stiff to move and the poor child was in a high fever. There was nothing for it but to keep her in bed and send for her foster-mother to nurse her. It was Lucia however who came, since her daughter was at work in the fields and was busy all day. When Giovanni came home from school he said

"The school-mistress says you ought to put arnica on your shoulder."

The girl threw off the coverlet that the remedy might at once be applied; but Giovanni was obliged to say, somewhat mortified:

"I have not got any arnica." They looked at

each other in silence ; and the boy went on : " I have not got any ; and I do not know what it is." And La Matta answered :

" I do not know." And she pulled the bed-clothes over her again

CHAPTER IV.

THE incidents mentioned in the last chapter took place when Giovanni had been at school only a few months. But as time went on and he made good progress, his companions began to regard him with admiration, tried to keep up with him, administering now and then a friendly thrashing to which he replied with cuffs and thumps that were apt to leave their mark on the recipient He learnt all their games and before long was their leader in them all. Jumping, running, catching and being caught, shouting with all the power of his boy's lungs — these delights were new to Giovanni, who until now had lived alone. He became so greedy of them that his

games with his school-fellows were not enough for
him, and when he got home, the doctor was no
sooner out of the house, than he tried to coax La
Matta into playing with him.

" Quicker! Quicker! catch me if you can!"
And the girl would take the smallest steps she
could with her long legs, because she saw that the
child was enchanted to think that she could not
overtake him.   Or he would harness her with her
back bent, her head down.

" You shall be my horse," he would say; then,
taking a run from the other end of the room, with
one leap he was astride.   The girl, who was but a
lank and feeble creature, bent like a spring under
the sudden weight and her ribs seemed likely to
crack.   Not unfrequently her eyes were full of
tears as she painfully straightened her overgrown
length and she exclaimed : "How heavy you are!"
with an admiring smile.

The Dottorino was not the man to neglect the
small mercies that Providence had granted him,
and he never sent anything away from table that
could pamper the appetite of his maid of all work.
Consequently La Matta grew and grew, but as
slender as a lath and so thin that it was grievous

to see her; particularly when she had been playing for any length of time with Giovanni; her
bones seemed positively to stand out and creak
with leanness, and she would sometimes throw
herself on the edge of the hearth and declare she
could run and play no more.

But then the little boy would exclaim: "Then
I will go and play with Rachel," and the girl
would start up like a dying ass at a kick from its
master, and be the first to say: " No, come along,
I want another game."

Rachel was the daughter of a small proprietor
who in that humble neighborhood was looked upon
as a perfect nabob. He had purchased an old bat-
tered castle from the impoverished lords of the
soil, for something under a hundred thousand
francs; a sort of fortress with turrets, and an
outer wall, and a moat, and a draw-bridge; and
there he had set up for a great man, with a
good cook, a newspaper, and a few friends, with
whom he drank and played cards, or, when the
weather was gloomy, discussed all the important questions of the day in domestic and foreign
politics.

The doctor was one of the most assiduous

visitors to the lord of the castle who rejoiced in
the very unlordly name of Pedrotti.

"The Dottorino knows the age of every bottle
of wine in my cellar," the great man would say;
and the doctor made them grow old very rapidly,
without any contradiction from the owner; in return for which forbearance he was always ready to
say: "How young our friend Pedrotti looks for a
man of forty!" taking from his years those he was
prepared to add on to his vintages. Such little
amenities, which ingratiate a guest with his Am-
phitrion, came as easily to the parish-doctor as
though he had lived at court for years. On political questions he was never pig-headed; whatever
his host's views were he was always ready to en-
dorse them. Then he never failed to know when
Pedrotti was in the humor for a hearty laugh, and
laid himself out to indulge him even at the sacrifice of his own dignity, and of other things besides.
In short, there could not be a more delightful
companion, and the lord of the castle, not ungrateful, would say:

"But why do you not bring Giovanni, doctor? The fine gentlemen of old were free enough
with their coin to keep themselves amused; and

though you amuse me for nothing, it is at any rate but fair that I should give you and your son a dinner now and then."

Giovanni dined in the kitchen, and after dinner he played with Rachel who was nearly of the same age as himself; and when he went home after dining at the castle he had fine stories for La Matta of the games they had had, and elaborate descriptions of the little girl's dolls and finery.

For a time La Matta had listened to all this and said nothing; but she had not taken any pleasure in hearing of all these fine things, and one day she retorted with a smile of triumph :

"But you cannot jump upon Rachel's back and make a horse of her !"

"No," said the boy, "she is too little and her frock is too nice."

"I am nearly fifteen," La Matta observed with a proud laugh, and she looked down on her shabby skirt with a glance of intense satisfaction.

When Rachel was nine years old she was sent to school at Novara and the dinners at the castle lost their charm for Giovanni. In the winter especially, when he could not go into the garden, he generally ended by going to sleep in one corner of the room and when he had to be waked there was scolding, grumbling, and kicks—all the fuss and difficulty that usually attend the waking of a lad from the bliss of his first sleep. To avoid these scenes Signor Pedrotti used to send him home as soon as dinner was over, then there were four hours that he must spend alone with La Matta. By way of passing the time he bethought himself of teaching her to read. The girl was quite ready to play at so quiet a game, and after several lessons she had mastered the letter O. Whether Giovanni wrote it or pointed it out in large print, she recognized O and repeated O, O, grinning with delight. But there was more difficulty with the other letters, and the lad, soon out of patience, wearied of the attempt and invented other amusements.

CHAPTER V.

FOUR years slipped away; Giovanni had gone through the four classes of the elementary school and all Fontanetto talked of his remarkable aptitude. But out there in the country there was no opportunity for further study.

"I cannot afford to send him to study at a great school; I will send him out to keep sheep, like the sons of the patriarchs," said his father very philosophically. But he did not waste his breath in saying this to the country louts; he knew too much not to be well aware of the value of breath, and he never spent it in vain. He said this to his richer neighbors. Signor Pedrotti, the height of whose ambition was a tricolor ribbon, understood that a merciful providence had here given him an opening for gaining credit among his neighbors as a generous and liberal-minded man. So one evening he proposed to the other magnates of the district that they should subscribe in equal proportions to bear the expense of sending "the poor

boy who had displayed so much intelligence," to
school. Six of them agreed and a convent of Lay
Friars was presently heard of at Novara, where
the terms were only forty francs a month, and the
teaching very good. When all was settled the six
patrons sent for the little doctor and Giovanni, and
Signor Pedrotti, taking up his parable, shed from
sublime heights their united beneficence on the
head, so to speak, of the beneficiary.

"To be rich is not enough," he said. "To
spend it liberally and judiciously, that is the important thing. This boy will be grateful to us all
his life for the benefit we are about to confer on
him. We will make a doctor of him to cure our
peasant children when the Dottorino here shall
have eaten his last dinner and ordered his last
pill."

The doctor laughed heartily at the joke, and
when their mirth had subsided the lord of the
castle proceeded to unfold the scheme . . . the convent, the forty francs a month, the four years of
schooling without holidays, the university education which would follow, etc., etc. The doctor's
expressions of gratitude were such as to satisfy
his patrons, who remarked, to his credit, that he

was not one of those poor but proud men who give themselves the airs of expatriated princes, so that you never know where to have them.

As to Giovanni, he knew several little shepherd boys who rolled down the slopes, slept on the grass, scampered over hill and dale and made holiday the livelong day ; and he would have preferred his father's original plan of sending him out to mind the sheep. But he was quite ready to adapt himself to the view that he was to become a doctor, beginning by going to school at Novara, and taking an altogether new start in life.

When the boy was gone the doctor's house was as silent as the tomb, and La Matta, contrary to all her former habits, took to neglecting her duties and spoiling her dishes, and would have become no more than a careless slattern if she had not had an energetic master, who at the cost of exciting his nerves and disturbing his bile, found means of correcting her which left their marks for a time and made her understand the necessity of taking pains with her work. Still, when she was alone she would often sit in ecstatic reverie, gazing at the chests and the tables over which the child had so often leaped, and she would smile to her-

self as if she could see him before her.   One day,
when by chance she raised her eyes to the baker's
shop and caught sight of an O in among the letters of his sign-board, she felt as pleased as though
she had met with an old friend; she repeated it
again and again, as if she could not tire of the
sound, and after that she looked at all the shop
signs and when she found an O would fix her
eyes on it quite lovingly, and then they would fill
with tears as if she had been gazing at the sun.

Sometimes, on a Sunday, she might go to see
her foster-mother, and if the doctor were dining out
she stayed to share the family polenta.   The foster-mother took no notice of her; in the open
season she was in the fields from dawn till sunset,
or carried baskets of stones down from the hills;
in the winter she sat spinning in the cow-shed till
midnight, and always had arrears of sleep to make
up, which stupefied her.   She made up for lost time,
to some extent, on Sundays, in church, where she
slept through the service.   Old Lucia, on the contrary, who did the house work, always had something to teach La Matta; on high festivals she
took her with her to church, and by dint of getting her to repeat the Latin prayers she had at

last succeeded in making her learn them by heart.
The girl did not understand a word of them, nor
the old woman either for that matter; but what
did that signify? so long as "the One above" understood ? And so La Matta devoutly repeated
her jumble of gibberish to persuade the Almighty
to bring Giovanni home again. Now and again
she would ask Lucia how much she had got laid
by in the savings bank, and then she went through
distracting calculations to find out whether she
had enough to buy a rocking-horse that Giovanni
had once coveted in a shop at Borgomanero.

After that rapid growth of late girlhood La
Matta grew no more; she remained at something
above the middle height of woman, but she never
grew fat. Her shoulders and hips were broad, but
they were bony, and she had none of that fullness
of curve which give grace and beauty to womanhood. She was dark, with an immense quantity
of coal-black hair, which by a copious application
of oil and pomatum she reduced to some approach
to smoothness. Her eyes too were black, large,
and deep-set, with long, thick lashes and heavy
eyebrows that met over the bridge of a short and
rather snub nose. Her high cheek-bones, powerful

jaw, and thick lips which showed her large white
teeth, gave her the appearance of a mulatto.
Within the memory of old Lucia there had been
at Novara a negro, in the service of a family of
rank who displayed this exotic specimen on the
foot-board of their state carriage. Lucia had her
suspicions that this negro was responsible for La
Matta's existence.

CHAPTER VI.

AT length Giovanni came home; but he
was so tall, and spoke in such a big voice, that La
Matta no longer dared to offer him the plaything
he had longed for. His education in the convent
had made him more shy than ever; he greeted his
father with no sort of effusion, and he scarcely
noticed the girl, just nodding to her and saying:
" Oh ! it is you !"

La Matta replied laughing, but with tears in
her eyes; and all the time she was in the kitchen,
getting the dinner ready, she laughed and cried
together repeating an imitation of that nod of

Giovanni's. She dared not address another word to him, and as she heard him speaking she kept saying to herself:

"Oh, Madonna Santa! Madonna Santa!" She could not convince herself that that tall figure, that voice and that conventual garb were those of the little boy who had so often jumped on her back in his romps.

Giovanni's patrons were curious to see their protégé, and all in turn asked him to dinner. At every house he met the very same company, and the same conversation repeated itself again and again: "They hoped that Giovanni was duly grateful for all the favors conferred upon him, since without his benefactors' generosity he would be to this day a peasant among paupers and sheep." . . . "Instead of which, here he was, a gentleman among gentlemen," added Signor Pedrotti with pregnant sarcasm, "for he sits with his elbows on the table and has not as yet said thank you to any one."

Giovanni colored, but he did not cease to be taciturn and clownish, or to knit his brows as if he were angry.

Signor Pedrotti was the last to give him that

solemn dinner, because he wished at the same time
to celebrate the return of his daughter Rachel
from school. When the Dottorino entered the
huge dining-room at the castle, the master of the
house was rocking himself in an American chair
near the glass doors that led into the garden.
They were open, and the sun, gliding in between
the leaves of the creepers of the verandah, danced
in chequered lights through the gloom of the in-
terior and sported on the walls and floor in disks
of every size, played in arabesques of light and
shade over the arabesques of the damask table-
cloth and drew sparks from the plate and glass
that were laid for dinner, while one steady ray fell
on Signor Pedrotti's manly breast and there ended
as though it had pierced him like a blade of polished steel.

It was a bright picture — a summer scene and
luxurious withal; it ought to have produced a
soothing effect on any one, especially after a walk
under a scorching August sun. But Giovanni did
not seem to feel it so; he hung back as if he hoped
to make his escape, and a hot flame of color rose
to his cheeks as he uneasily gripped his hat — the
cocked hat of the Order of Lay Friars. At a cor-

ner of the table, straight, fresh, and smiling, he saw
Rachel, the companion of his childish sports, over
whom he had been wont to domineer with all the
tyranny of superior strength and daring, and who
now quelled him by the power of her superior
position and beauty. She was plainly dressed in
the uniform of her school — a cambric frock with
a wide pleated frill, and she had stuck a scarlet
verbena flower in her hair; but her brilliant color-
ing and slim figure gave the simple dress a fitness
that looked like luxury. Her complexion had that
dazzling whiteness and rosiness that in a very
young girl are enough to make her beautiful, or at
any rate to make her seem so. Her hair was of a
rich gold color, her eyes blue, her lips scarlet; it
was one of those bright-hued faces which strike
at first sight and by the side of which the hand-
somest brunette is eclipsed.

"My daughter," said Signor Pedrotti with
pride, and the Dottorino, after declaring that she
was an angel, sang with an air of gallantry:

"*Sei tu dal ciel discesa, o in ciel son io con
te?*"* and Signor Pedrotti laid down his newspaper
to laugh the more at his ease.

* Art thou come down from Heaven, or am I in Heaven with thee?

But while the doctor, pressing his hands to his heart and giving himself operatic airs, repeated the refrain: "*Son io, son io, o in ciel son io, son io con te,*" his eyes fell on his unworthy son, who had shrunk, blushing deeply, in his grotesque priest's uniform, as close as he could squeeze himself against the door-post, as if he were trying to vanish into the wall. It is disappointing when a man has been so lucky as to make himself popular with all his neighbors to find his only offspring so degenerate that he cannot even appreciate his father's graces, much less imitate them ; and the Dottorino, wounded in his paternal soul at perceiving that Giovanni seemed mortified rather than radiant at finding himself there with him, went up to him and nipping him by the ear said :

" Come here, you bear, and kiss your benefactor's hand, and pay your respects to his daughter, your benefactress."

But Giovanni in his awkwardness had no idea how to perform the ceremony required of him. He turned redder than ever, till the veins on his forehead stood out and his eyes felt as if they would start out of his head, and he drew back, without a word or scarcely a bow. The doctor

who felt that it was now his part to make com-
pensation to his patron for this school-boy loutish-
ness, gave him an indignant shove saying: "Go,
you young cub; I could not believe that you were
a son of mine."

Giovanni stumbled against the table, making a
great tingling and clatter; then, recovering his
balance, he stood stock-still, without even raising
his eyes; but his hands shook and his lips quivered,
and he had turned as pale as if he had suddenly·
lost every drop of blood in his body.

"Let him alone, Dottore," said Signor Pedrotti,
shrugging his shoulders. "He has been badly
brought up, but he has plenty of brains and in time
he will know better. We will make a great man
of him yet."

The other guests now began to arrive; they
admired Rachel, paid their compliments, talked
loud, discussed the news, and Signor Pedrotti repeated the doctor's neat sentiment: "*Sei tu dal
ciel discesa, o in ciel son io, son io con te. . .*" at
which every one laughed, and clapped and applauded the doctor's pretty wit; only Giovanni
stood immovable by the table, awkward, uncomfortable, pushed against by one, stared at by an-

other who laughed at him to his face — neglected
and despised by all. Rachel, however, looked at
him with compassion, and no sooner had her father
and the others fairly started a conversation among
themselves than she went up to the lad and said:

"Would you like to go out into the garden for
a little while ?"

He half raised his eyes, glanced at the space
between himself and the verandah, and seeing that
it was crowded with his benefactors, he rushed
past them, without saying a word, without turning
round, out of the glass door, and only stopped
when he was fairly outside; thankful to find himself out of that room.

Rachel had followed him, and, like him, was
somewhat discomposed by this little scene.

"All the roses are over," she said, pulling a
few leaves from a rose-bush near at hand. "Do
you see how that medlar tree is loaded with
fruit ?"

And as she spoke she went slowly forward
looking round at Giovanni as though to suggest
that he should accompany her. He followed her;
but he still felt his humiliation and could hardly
manage to reply that indeed there was a great

quantity of fruit. Then, hearing the dinner bell, he turned to go in again, as if he were in a hurry to escape.

Some of the company had their children with them, and Signor Pedrotti had had a separate table laid for the young people and for Giovanni. Rachel, to whom her father pointed out a place at the bigger table, said to the lad :

" We must ask you to be so kind as to keep an eye on these young gentlemen, or who knows what mischief they might not be at," and she pointed to a chair that had its back to the grown-up company, where he would escape inspection and comment.

Giovanni felt a genuine relief at finding himself thus isolated, and he thanked her simply and not in the least awkwardly; and after the meal, during which, being out of sight he was also out of mind, when the whole party were bustling in and out of the garden with the coffee cups, he went up to Rachel and asked her whether she had enjoyed her dinner.

" Very much thank you ; and you ?"

" Oh ! I was most comfortably placed," exclaimed Giovanni gratefully. " Thank you a

thousand times for having put me with the little
ones."

There was a short silence ; then he went on
again : "Will you say good-night to your father
for me ; I do not wish to disturb him." And he
hurried away as if he were flying from the spot.

La Matta was astonished to see him return so
early, for the sun was still high; and she muttered,
as was her habit: "He likes being at home better
than going to the castle."

She stood gazing for some minutes at the door
of the room into which Giovanni had retreated;
and then exclaimed with a sigh : "What a pity it
is that he never plays any games now!" And
that evening she did not go out to gossip with her
neighbors.

Rachel had any number of relations at Borgomanero, at Boca, at Maggiore, at Orta ; she was
always driving about with her father and paying
visits, and the Dottorino had been too deeply
humiliated by his son's behavior at the castle ever
to wish to take him there again on the few occasions when its proprietor, in the intervals of his
visits, invited him to dine there.

"Never again till he has shed the garb and

the manners of a Lay Friar, will you see him here
with me," the doctor said to Rachel when she en-
quired for him.

CHAPTER VII.

THE vacation came to an end and Giovanni went to Turin to study at the university
without seeing the companion of his childhood
any more.   But he no sooner made a friend than
he talked to him of her and of the delights of
their childish play; and then he would describe
how she had grown up during the years when he
was at school; expatiate on her beauty, her grand
air and her dignified demeanor.   Still, the whole
truth as to their one and only meeting he never
had the courage to confess; not even the fact as
to his luckless conventual dress; he preferred to
be communicative on the subject of his dreams
and hopes.   His ecclesiastical garments were now
shed and left behind with the memories of school
and his loutish timidity; the life of the university,
the adoption of a dress like everybody else, the

liking of his acquaintances and the consideration
which his talents did not fail to gain for him, were
pleasing to his naturally bold spirit.   Notwithstanding his intense admiration for Rachel, he did
not fail to throw himself into all the pleasures that
surrounded him ; and so far as the narrow limits
of his purse allowed, he was ready to pay for his
experience of life.   He was eager to rid himself of
his awkwardness, his simplicity, and the novice-
like bashfulness of which he was so much ashamed.
He must be handsome, smart, elegant, to present
himself before her ; he must learn to talk with
ease and ready wit, and must have passed his ex-
aminations in such a way as to promise well for his
future.

He would say to his friend :   " Look at so and
so, who is now delegate of a college and who has
written this or that — he is the son of a dairy-
woman ; and so and so, who is now a minister,
was a tailor's apprentice."   And then he would
mention Rossini, Beethoven, Haydn, and above
all Shakespeare ; he felt that he too could rise.

" I will be a great lawyer like Brofferio.* — I
will make fifty thousand francs a year.   Crowds

* Brofferio was then at the height of his glory.

shall come to hear me conduct a case, all Fontanetto will want to be there. . . ."

But at this time he said nothing about marriage ; life was no less than a love-poem ; Rachel
should learn to feel the same admiration for his
talents, for his triumphs of eloquence, for his
glory, as he felt for her beauty. He said of her with
ingenuous sincerity: "She is so white and fair and
her clothes are so sweet and seemly, her ways and
actions are so delightful, that it all goes to one's
head ; I hardly dare speak to her, it seems too
bold ; she is made of superior stuff to us. I blushed
to hear my own big voice after hearing her speak,
and was ashamed of my own clumsiness as I
watched her move so softly and gracefully. I felt
as though if I held her hand I should leave the
mark of my fingers on it; but indeed I should as
soon think of doing such a thing as I should of
shaking hands with the queen."

Or he would point out some lady passing in
her carriage : "There. She is like that — only
fresher ; and like that — only fairer ; and like
that—only. . ." And the third had some defect,
or lacked some perfection. But he did not feel
that any such gulf yawned between him and these

fine ladies as parted him from Rachel. It never
occurred to him that he was measuring the distance under more favorable circumstances.

Autumn came, and with it the long vacation;
and Giovanni went home to Fontanetto. When
the lord of the castle informed his daughter that
the student was in the neighborhood and that he
had invited him to dine on the next day, Rachel
exclaimed compassionately:

"Oh dear, papa, could you not have left him
alone? He is so shy that he is miserable when
he is with other people."

"Yes, he is shy, and it becomes him," replied
Pedrotti. "I cannot endure a forward lad. He
knows his position and keeps his place. This shows
that he has good sense, and if he always behaves
so he will get on; well, we shall see. For at any
rate I shall give him a place at the children's table
that he may take no nonsense into his head; I
have asked our friends to bring their children on
purpose, as they did last year."

Rachel was satisfied; sure now of having
secured her old friend a position where he would
be spared humiliation, she breathed more freely,
saying:

"Nothing could be better," and she went about her duties as mistress of the house.

She dressed with as much simplicity as ever ; a light muslin frock with no flouncing or frilling, quite independent of the prevailing fashion ; a neat crimped collar, such as she had always worn at school, a little white apron edged with lace, and a flower in her hair. And she came down-stairs smiling and received the first arrivals with many blushes and some reserve but without awkwardness, and with the ease and grace that were natural to her. From time to time she glanced out at the court-yard, a little anxious as to Giovanni's first appearance. . .Would there be a repetition of the scene of last year ? She wished to avert that but did not know what to do.

CHAPTER VIII.

THE doctor was late. Signor Pedrotti began to glance at the clock on the chimney-piece and to count the five-minutes as they passed. The company had already done more than allude to the quarter of an hour's grace after which no one could ever be expected to wait, and had taken to wandering up and down the room, inspecting the names laid on the napkins, glancing at the pictures, drumming on the window panes, talking spasmodically and demeaning themselves like spirits in torment. A storm was evidently brewing which would not fail to fall on the head of the hapless scape-goat. Rachel foreseeing it pulled a few flowers out of the large bunch that decorated the centre table and put them into a smaller vase which she set in the middle of the children's table; in the kindliness of her soul, she thought she was providing some amends for the rebuffs under which the hapless victim was doomed to suffer. While she was still leaning busily over the table, she heard a pleasant voice with a clear ring in it like the upper notes of a tenor, which said :

" We are very late I am afraid. I found that my father did not come in, so I came on to make our excuses. . ."

Rachel turned round in surprise and saw at once that the little priestling of the past year had developed into the handsome young man who stood before her; but Giovanni had trusted too much to his presence of mind, and when he found himself face to face with her he turned scarlet. He did not dare hold out his hand, but paused at some little distance, bowing low and trying to think of something to say, some address which should not be absolutely commonplace—but without success. All that suggested itself was simply this:

" How do you do, Signorina; I hope you are well ?"

He had grown a great deal, and was of a very good height, straight and well built. His neck was long and his head small; his hair was black, thick, and curly, his eyes dark and deep-set, his cheek bones were rather strongly marked and had a bright patch of color below the eyes, such as an

actor puts on to give brilliancy to his glance. And
his look was in fact fiery and eager, with a sparkle
that gave the lie to his bashfulness if it did not
entirely conceal it. His lips, again, were brightly
red and dewy, his teeth large and white, with a
most engaging smile — an attractive mouth altogether, which it was a pity to think should ever be
hidden under a moustache. He was, in short, a
remarkably handsome young fellow; but beauty,
which is often a snare to a man, sat lightly on him
because he was perfectly unconscious of it, or at
least he did not regard it as ground for vanity.
He still thought himself far beneath Rachel, and
his fixed purpose was to raise himself to her level
by his talents, by steady work, by the hardest and
most difficult means — and not by good looks.

"Very well, thank you, Signor Giovanni, and
you?" replied Rachel, slightly dashed and blushing as deeply as himself. But these simple words
gave Giovanni the keenest pleasure, because they
were said in a way that suggested to his mind
that the companion of his childhood had begun to
feel a little conscious in his presence — that he was
man enough for her to blush at his address as she
would at that of any other man.

While these brief salutations were being uttered the Dottorino arrived, and all the party
sought their places at the table. Rachel did not
know what to say to this elegant young gentleman
who was to be put to sit with the children ; and she
remained standing between the two tables in the
greatest embarrassment. But Giovanni, who had
not altogether got rid of his shyness, and was still
delighted to escape the intolerable patronage of
his benefactors, made an effort to reassure Rachel
and himself.

"I hope," he said, and his voice was slightly
tremulous, "that I am not to be separated from
my little friends. We made acquaintance last
year. . ."

The little ones stared with open eyes and
mouths ; they did not recognize this grand gentleman. Giovanni seated himself among them
and proceeded to help them. He cut up the meat
on their plates, gave them each a piece of
bread, and then tried to recall himself to their remembrance.

"Once upon a time there were six little children. . ." and he went on to describe their various
tricks, making each in his turn feel a little ashamed ;

"and there was one boy much bigger than they were, dressed like a priest with a long gown like this, and a hat like this. . ." and he sketched a caricature of himself.

The children then remembered him and there was such laughing and chattering and merriment that at the other table they could not hear each other speak for the noise. The doctor's jokes, which for thirty years had never failed of success, could not raise the faintest titter. And so by degrees the solemn discussion of political or municipal affairs was given up, and all these grave dignitaries — members of the town or of the Provincial Council, and secretaries of parochial boards were sitting with their heads and ears turned to the children's table, only too glad when they caught a few words that supplied a clue to the cause of all this mirth. Signor Pedrotti, however, did not take this sudden metamorphosis in his protégé with so good grace as his colleagues. His view of things was that he should always be visibly and obviously the patron, shedding the condescending dew of encouragement on a youth unconscious of his own value, and having all the credit himself of discovering an unappreciated genius. He expected that Giovanni should be so overcome by reverence and respect as not to dare speak in his presence without being first spoken to; and the lad's newly-acquired independence seemed to him a lack of deference. He thought he would have him under his own eye to keep him in order so he said with sòme irony:

"Since you are so merry there come here; come and make us laugh too."

Giovanni, in the strictness of his rectitude had all the inexperience of eighteen, he felt the offensiveness of this speech, as though his patron had said: "Come and play the fool," and had added: "as your father does."

Now, to play the parasite as his father did was the thing he held in the greatest horror; he was always on his guard against it, and was defiant in sheer dread of being servile. However, he rose to obey, but he registered a vow to himself that he would not "lend himself to the mean part of a buffoon."

The seat which was offered to him was, as it happened, next to Rachel; perhaps because it became her, as mistress of the house, to make room. But the guests at the upper

table were none the gayer for Giovanni's joining their circle. He was on the defensive, and
became very reserved and serious, as beseemed a
young gentleman among his seniors. He opened
a conversation with his young hostess on books
and reading; and being strictly classical, a purist
and a puritan in matters of taste, he ran down the
modern school, and raved about *i Promessi Sposi*,
especially enlarging on the improvements in the
second edition. Rachel had read Manzoni's novel
at school, but she had heard nothing about the
editions, and knew of no difference between them;
so, thinking to make herself agreeable to her
guest, she said she had read the first and desired
nothing better than to make herself acquainted
with the second; expressing her ardent regrets at
having reached the age of discretion in ignorance
of the correct version of *i Promessi Sposi*. Giovanni eagerly offered to lend it to her, and she accepted with no less eager acknowledgements.

But Signor Pedrotti interposed :

"What need," said he, "could there be for a
second edition ?"

The literary discussion was quite out of the ordinary groove of ideas at Fontanetto, and disturbed

the philosophy of the lord of the castle. He regarded all literary folk as a useless and idle crew, he could not understand how any one should spend money on books, "which, even if you read them, are no manner of good when once they have been read," and he exclaimed in solemn tones: "Good Heavens! How can such people earn enough to live on?" adding sternly: "They would do better to work for their bread."

When he came in from walking through his fields and plantations he would take up the newspaper for which he subscribed, and say as he unfolded it: "Now let us see how geese are crammed."

This was a joke of the Dottorino's that Pedrotti had appropriated some ten years since, and which the doctor never failed to applaud as a brilliant flash of original wit.

When he had disposed of the *Promessi Sposi* Signor Pedrotti turned to the lady next to him and remarked with a roguish air:

"I had my table made a metre longer this summer, but before I have the pleasure of receiving my friends again I must have the doors made wider." This was a facetious allusion to the crinolines, and of course every one laughed at his wit; while the doctor hummed the refrain of a song that was just then popular at Novara comparing the clouds of skirts that were in fashion to the tail of a comet, and they all laughed again.

Then they talked about the comet, which was the great event of the season; and told stories of the superstitions of the peasants. It was an omen of ill, of an epidemic, of a great war, or a famine — etc., etc. — But in spite of the laughter there was a shade of uneasiness on some faces — suppose the peasants were right after all !

"Old Castalda," said Pedrotti, "told me the other evening that the comet swept the courtyard with its great tail; and fell to crying: 'The worse for us, whatever shall we poor mortals do ?' I asked her why. 'Don't you see,' she said, 'it will sweep away the harvest.' What an idea. Ha, ha, ha !"

He expected a response from the doctor, and seeing him intent on his conversation with his neighbor he called out to him: "Do you hear, Dottorino, the comet is to sweep away the harvest !"

"Indeed ! I should be glad to have all that is

left after the sweeping," the doctor hastened to reply, having made the same remark at home. This
answer satisfied Pedrotti, who was always flattered
by any suggestion that others wanted or wished
for anything he possessed. He led the laugh, and
indeed, at this rate, there was no reason why they
should cease to laugh for the rest of the evening.

Meanwhile the choicer souls had found themselves in perfect agreement Just opposite Giovanni sat the wife of the secretary to the town
council who took no part in the general diversion.
She was a woman of about forty; tall, thin and
fair, but so sunburnt as to look at a distance fresh
and rosy, thus encouraging her pretensions to ju-
venility. She always sat with downcast eyes; always spoke with her lips pursed up, and so sour
an expression that she seemed to spite everybody;
but as a matter of fact she was always saying kind
and even pretty speeches: "Rachel dear, you
look as fresh as a flower to-day," but in a tone
that might have implied: "What on earth in-
duced you to dress yourself such a figure?"

Then she had a mania for singing the most la-
mentable and time-honored songs:

4 *

"*Non mi chiamate più biondina bella.*"

And here the doctor invariably whispered to his next neighbor that it was many years since any one had thought of such a thing.

"*Chiamatemi biondina sventurata.*"*

This lady began a sentimental discourse on music for Giovanni's benefit.

"I *feel* music," she began, "I feel it so deeply that I suffer under it. It always makes me cry. Last year, on the lake of Orta, we went out one night in a boat and played and sang by moonlight. A flute — oh how delicious the tone of a flute is!

"*Io t'amerò finchè le rondinelle!*"

Giovanni, finding himself treated for the first time in his life as a man, and taken into the confidence of a lady of so much importance, thought he could not do better than agree entirely with her sentiments on music. He quoted vehemently from an article he had read in a Milan newspaper, and declaimed against Wagner—a tirade to which the lady listened with no more than the vaguest comprehension. He talked rather loudly to give

---

* "Call me no longer fair and beautiful, call me henceforth, alas, the hapless fair."

himself courage and also to seem quite at his ease, making rather a display of his contempt for the frivolous subjects that were occupying the attention of the rest of the company, and defiantly keeping his share of the conversation on the higher level of art and literature, as much as to say: "This is my element; and I cannot descend to your petty interests."

At last Pedrotti lost patience:

"It seems to me," he said, "that you think rather too much of politics, and music, and things that do not concern you. You would do better to leave the fine arts to finer folks and attend a little more to your studies, or all the sacrifices that have been made for you will be thrown away."

Giovanni, who had colored, turned pale with rage. And he was on the point of replying indignantly, but at that instant Rachel placed a dish of bonbons before him and asked him with a smile to take one.

"Thanks," said he, but without attending ; .and he put out a tremulous hand to pass the dish to his neighbor and utter the retort he had on the tip of his tongue. But Rachel insisted.

"You will not refuse me?" said she.

No, he did not refuse, he took one — the first that came, and again put out his hand to pass the dish. She, however, recommended a different variety; a chocolate bonbon. He was forced to accept and to thank her.

Signor Pedrotti meanwhile had plunged into another subject; he was discussing the fluctuation of wealth; to which the doctor with his unfailing readiness contrasted the stability of poverty, a joke which, happening to be new, produced a dazzling effect. Giovanni at length saw that Rachel's manœuvre had been intended only to avert a war of words between her father and himself; and he thought it a miracle of readiness and tact. "She is a perfect lady," he thought to himself, and he felt more ashamed than ever of his timidity and of his affected boldness. He desired above all things to be a real and perfect gentleman; but he saw that he fell short of it, and he no longer dared to assert his pretensions. Face to face with Rachel he felt his smallness and was humiliated. He would have been only too glad if he could have achieved some heroic adventure to raise himself in the young girl's estimation; but, in reality, he scarcely dared to say half a dozen words to her, nor did he venture to offer her his hand when he took leave ; though ever since he had come in, nay even before, he had been burning to do so.

Rachel herself was as gracious and kind as she could be over their parting; and when she was alone, just before going to rest, she sat down on the edge of the bed, slightly pensive as she remembered that only the day before she had exchanged a few jesting speeches with a young lawyer of the town, a man of about thirty who had seemed disposed to pay her some attention ; and a sudden disgust, a blind impulse of rage surged up in her soul against that young man ; if he had been by, she could have slapped him.

CHAPTER IX.

DURING the days that followed Rachel could not get the thought of Giovanni out of her head; the lad's eager speech had made a great impression on her. He must certainly be wonderfully familiar with art and letters to be able to talk like that. Her father was an old man and lived buried in a village; he was incapable of appreciating him; that young fellow was really immensely clever...

Then as she thought of the mortifications to which his patrons had subjected him, her blood boiled; she felt that their injustice and cruelty were quite preposterous. The slightest allusion to the allowance they made him she felt as an insult, and in her eyes Giovanni was one of society's victims — a noble victim, enduring his torture with a dignity that was nothing less than sublime, curbing his youthful ardor of indignation and smothering his justifiable pride out of respect for his seniors. She idealized him into a martyr and a hero.

She had guessed, too, that he loved her, and she was proud of it; every time they happened to meet she was prepared for "a declaration," and when that should come she promised herself that she would make up to him for all the humiliations he had endured. This was a bold scheme, for which she could find no precedent in the few love stories she had read, nor in the confidences of her school friends; in these the young girl invariably repulsed the first whispers of a lover, and only responded to the second. Now, she had determined to answer at once: "Yes, I love you, because you are poor and unfortunate, and I am ready to share your poverty and your misfortunes."

And so, anticipating this "declaration," she did her utmost to perform the part of a love-sick maiden. She would say very frankly: "I cannot bear people who are rich and ignorant. I will never marry any but a man of talent. The poverty of genius is a noble poverty; all the greatest men have been poor."

Then she was always talking of Giovanni; not that she ever felt bold enough to utter his name— she spoke of him as the doctor's son, and her friends would say: "You are in love with that doctor's son."

Her chivalrous partisanship never led her to the length of confessing this openly, but in her childish quixotism she was very well content that it should be guessed at. Her father contemned this young fellow while she loved him; it was an indemnification. She carried this sentimentality into everything she did; she adopted a motto which she wrote at the top of her note-paper, and on her music, and in her books; in short, everywhere: "Poor and destitute art thou, O philosophy!"

Then she took a fancy to that imbecile invention, the language of flowers, of which schoolgirls are so fond, and always wore a symbolical blossom in her dress; flowers sometimes so strange as to invite inquiry. For a time she always displayed a tulip, meaning *a declaration of love* — the declaration she was expecting from Giovanni; then, she appeared with a carnation pinned head downwards.

"Why do you wear your pink upside down?"

"It stands for *unrequited love*."

One day, when she felt very desperate, she

stuck a thistle into her dress that pricked her friends when they embraced her. This was the emblem of *grief.* She worked herself the most wonderful collars, on which, instead of the usual arabesques or lace patterns, she embroidered pansies with a sentimental motto, or doves with a note in their beaks with some illegible posy; all of which was labor lost, since the minuteness of the work made the intention invisible; as to Giovanni, he lived too retired a life for the gossip of the girls, who understood all these whimsicalities, ever to reach his ears.

He, for his part, shut himself up with his flame, smarting under his inferior position. During these vacation months he spent the greater part of the day in solitary wanderings across the country, thinking, dreaming, building endless castles in the air. He dreamed of a time when he should have finished his studies and achieved something great; something — what precisely he did not know — his visions varied with the mood he was in or the books he had last read. One day he would dream of the triumph of some grand dramatic piece, another of gaining some great case as a pleader ; or of bringing out a book which should be applauded by all the critics, or of being unanimously elected deputy, and returned as member to parliament by the devotion and respect of the whole district; then he would have succeeded in carrying some important measure, against all hope, by a splendid display of parliamentary eloquence. Sometimes again his dreams were of battle, and of heroic courage; he saw himself wounded, decorated on the field, and promoted to high rank — the man on whom the eyes of Italy were fixed. And when he had reached the crowning glory of his dream he threw himself at Rachel's feet saying: " I have done all this only to make myself worthy of you."

The Rachel of his visions always received him kindly, tenderly, nay, with gratitude — they were alone in those dreams, and mastered by his passion, she yielded to his embrace and confessed that she—yes, she too, had always loved him, and that she had waited because her faith in him had never failed.

At length he became so entirely absorbed in these imaginings that he avoided meeting any one for fear of interrupting them; he had created a world of illusion in which he was exquisitely

happy, in that haven of bliss his shyness and lout-
ishness caused him no embarrassment or blushes;
he saw himself as he would like to be, and he was
content. By degrees he persuaded himself that
this phantom existence had its foundation in reality; that Rachel knew all about it since, in it, he
told her everything; and he ceased to regard it
as a fabric of his fancy, but thought of it as a
secret in which she was a sharer.

One evening, as he was going up the hill, he
met Rachel with a party who were coming down
from seeing the vineyard. She felt herself color,
she lost the thread of the sentence she was uttering, and was altogether so much agitated by seeing him that she dared not raise her eyes, and
barely greeted him with a slight bow. In point
of fact—setting aside the circumstance of her
being in love with him — there was no reason why
this young lady, the only child and heiress of the
richest proprietor in the district, should bow at all
more effusively to this impecunious student; but
Giovanni had so merged their two lives in his love
dreams, had made himself so completely one with
her, that at last he had persuaded himself that
there was a real chain between them, and her dis-

tant greeting had the effect on his nerves of a drenching from head to foot with a pail of cold water; it startled him as something extraordinary —it was an infidelity, a desertion. He was sore and unhappy; he went over all his reasons for thinking that Rachel loved him : the flowers that she had placed before him with her own hands when he had sat at the side-table; the sweatmeat she had pressed upon him to save him from his skirmish with her father. . . . These were all; but on these slender materials, followed by her cold bow, he constructed a whole romance of love and faithlessness, in which he played the interesting part of the victim ; and the next morning, happening to be Sunday, he went to church and seating himself at the end of Signor Pedrotti's seat, in the attitude affected by disconsolate lovers, he kept his eyes fixed on Rachel throughout the service with a mournful and reproachful gaze, which disturbed Rachel greatly.

CHAPTER X.

WHEN Giovanni was about to return to college he was once more bidden to dine with Signor Pedrotti. The doctor was jubilant as he delivered this invitation. A good dinner was always a joyful event in his eyes. Giovanni, on the contrary, was painfully excited, and indulged in the wildest schemes and visions which deprived him of sleep. Thus, the next day, when the time came to make his appearance at his patron's house he was quite exhausted by having lain awake all night with his thoughts, in a fevered alternation of lovers' day-dreams — indignation, reproaches, reconciliation — over which he had shed torrents of hot tears in the confidence of his pillow. This time he was very certain that he must utter the secret which was tormenting him; he thought that after all he had suffered it would be easier to speak than to be silent.

"Why did she bow so coldly? How have I offended her? Has she forgotten that she placed

those flowers for me on the side-table? Can she
think that I could fail to understand what she
meant by those flowers? They were a confession,
a promise. . ." And he felt as though he were
actually pouring all this out to Rachel herself who
could not — did not, wonder — after all that had
passed between them.

But, as often occurs with castle-builders, all
his visions vanished at the first touch of reality.
He no sooner saw the table laid, the customary
guests, the regular force of children, Rachel's face
with its polite smile, than he knew he had dreamed
dreams, and that there was nothing between him
and the young girl that was not perfectly commonplace. The discovery mortified him; he was dis-
couraged, dejected, and took no pains to seem at
his ease as he had on the previous occasion. Seeing him sit with his eyes cast down, silent, and
eating nothing, Signor Pedrotti felt that he could
forgive his protégé and he had no objection to re-
sume the role of patron, to give him some encouragement, and to predict a brilliant future for
the lad.

"You must become a great man and justify
the confidence I have shown in you. I shall

have the glory of having discovered a hidden jewel. . . ."

When the lord of the castle pitched his address in this key Giovanni did in fact feel much encouraged, not only with regard to his career in life, but in his hopes of love for Rachel.

" If he has confidence in me. . ." thought he— and the bitterness, the insolence, the mortification under which he had smarted vanished from his memory.

The Dottorino, always eager to amuse his host, played the jester as usual, and by the end of dinner the company had become so jolly that the presence of a young girl was inconvenient; indeed, that of a lad whose experience of life was as yet an unknown quantity to them, rather paralyzed the merriment of the older men. The whole party went to take their coffee under the verandah, and Pedrotti said to the two young people :

" Just go and see that the little ones do not get into mischief and climb up the terrace bank."

The lovers went as they were bidden, without looking at each other. The way from the verandah to the terrace was along a straight path over- .

arched with creepers; they were still under the
eye of their elders; but above all they were in-
tensely conscious of each other's presence.

The dinner had been a long business, and in
autumn the days are short; it was growing dusk,
the terrace at the bottom of the garden looked out
over the plain, and the sun which was rapidly setting, had already sunk behind the hills at the back
of the castle. The children, disturbed at their play,
ran up a side path and continued their game a little way off and the two young people stood leaning over the parapet of the terrace. The fields
were deserted and silent; hardly a cricket or a
cicala was to be heard prolonging its shrill chirp
after the noisy concert of its hushed companions, or a
frog croaking from time to time in the pond, with
the chattering of the children in the upper path.
The waters of the Sissone, at some little distance,
made a sound like a saw. The balustrade was
overgrown by a Virginia creeper and the leaves,
though they had not yet fallen, had turned bright
red. It struck Giovanni that it was just here that
he had dreamed of making his confession and
clasping Rachel to his heart in an ecstasy of
love.

He looked at her — so strange to him, so dignified and so handsome, and his vision seemed
nothing less than preposterous. He was ashamed
at the mere remembrance of it, and he wanted to
make some commonplace remark for fear that
Rachel should guess his madness; but he did not
know what to say. Under the verandah they could
see the tiny lightning of the fusees, and then they
died out and the steady sparks of the men's cigars
burnt, like fiery eyes that watched them from afar.
A loud laugh reached their ears, and all that
Giovanni could find to say in an agitated tone
was:

" How they are laughing !"

Rachel made no reply but "yes," and she
smiled at her companion, as though to qualify the
abruptness of the monosyllable. As their eyes
met Giovanni remembered how he had looked at
her in church, and the same feelings came over
him, but minus the courage to speak which had
then fired his spirit. Rachel too had blushed
crimson, and she bent forward to gaze at the view
and hide her glowing color. Giovanni perceived
that she was experiencing some new sensation
now that she was alone with him; he looked at

her and trembled.   Rachel's blushes and agitation
were caused by him — they were for him — and
they should not elude him as his dreams had done.
Still, he could find nothing to say, indeed he was
not sure that he could command his voice to
speak.   Those starry cigars disturbed him, and
every now and then one of the little ones would
rush at him and throw its arms round his knees
and hide behind his legs, while the pursuer skip-
ped round him shouting with glee.   All this disconcerted him and jarred upon him, and meanwhile his heart was beating wildly, his throbbing
pulses deafened him, and he felt his senses failing
him as if he were fainting.   He took one step
towards Rachel as though to exclaim: 'I love
you," but a sudden gush of tears welled up in his
heart; he did not speak but bent his face over the
marble parapet, sobbing as if he were broken-
hearted.

Rachel looked round.   "Giovanni! oh what
is the matter?" she asked, but her voice too was
choked with tears.

That instant all his doubts were solved.   Giovanni drew himself up with flashing eyes and
flaming cheeks: "The matter is that I am a

fool — a madman. . ." he began with a passionate
impulse.

Two of the children came tearing down upon
them, laughing and shrieking, and drove them
against the balustrade; and all the glittering
cigars danced before his eyes.

" That — that. . ." he went on in a low voice,
and he came to a full stop.

There they stood, side by side, with their
heads bent; but he held out his hand to her for
the first time to say good-night, and Rachel gave
him hers. They were both as cold as ice and
both trembling. Giovanni grasped her fingers
with a desperate grip; then, in a voice as thick
and tremulous as that of a drunkard, he said:

" I cannot tell you what is the matter," and he
fled, almost running, till he was within reach of
those cigars which seemed ready to consume
him.

Later in the evening, when he was away from
the young girl, walking home along the dark
lanes with his father who stumbled and tottered
in his gait, Giovanni was seized with a sort of fury
against himself, calling himself an idiot, and shedding tears of rage to think that he should have let

such an opportunity slip without saying all that
weighed on his heart; and now it would be a whole
year before he could see Rachel again. And Rachel,
at the same hour, had locked herself into her
room, dissolved in tears, and crying for pardon to
the young man for having failed to find some kind
word of consolation, for having stood there like a
simpleton or a woman devoid alike of heart and
sense. They loved each other and they knew it,
and what more can two souls want in this world
to make them happy — and they were both
miserable.

CHAPTER XI.

MANY a time when he was away in Turin Giovanni felt a passionate desire to write to Rachel.
But he knew that she could not receive a letter by
post without the risk, or indeed the certainty, of
discovery. The post-office official of Fontanetto
was the baker, who also dealt in groceries and
hardware; his wife and daughter took the greatest
interest in all the letters that came and went; they

knew the handwriting and correspondents of all
the gentry in the neighborhood, and it was quite
beyond all hoping that a letter from Turin, addressed to Signorina Pedrotti, should pass through
their hands without giving rise to gossip and enquiry, even before it reached the castle. All the
same he could not resist the impulse to express
on paper the fever that was devouring his heart:
" I love you, Rachel; with all the ardor of a first
passion; I love you, and my love is hopeless.
Tell me that you love me — say only once that
you love me. . ." And he found a comfort in hearing his own voice as he read the vehement appeal
aloud, again and again. Sometimes, instead of
writing, he would read some appropriate epistles
from *la Nouvelle Heloise,* or *les Confessions d'un
Enfant du Siècle* or *Jacopo Ortis,* and he could
have believed that he had written them himself
and was in all the misery that they expressed, so
utterly melancholy was he under the influence of
his suppressed passion. Then he would read the
answers of the hapless ladies to whom they were
addressed, and pity Rachel as if the letters were
hers and insuperable obstacles stood between her
and her lover.

The autumn holidays however brought him a less romantic vein of ideas. It was an eventful year in Fontanetto; a grand festival was to be held, in honor of the transfer thither of the sacred body of St. Alexander. All the authorities and all the squireens had their houses filled with guests who sat round their hospitable boards by dozens, while superfluous covers were laid for unexpected visitors. Strangers poured in from every town within reach, even from Novara. At the castle were two ladies, a mother and daughter, from Milan, and with them a Swiss. The Swiss lady was the governess, but Signor Pedrotti did not like that this should be known and he introduced her to every one with an important air, as if she were some great personage who had come all the way from Zurich, and rushed to Fontanetto, to do honor to the bones of St. Alexander, and the savory meats prepared in the castle kitchen.

The festival lasted three days; but it kept the whole country side in excitement all through the month of August and even longer.

There is greater individual freedom at a dinner of fifty people than at one of ten, no doubt. Giovanni and Rachel soon found themselves practically téte-à-tête in the midst of the noisy crowd. The surroundings however were not sufficiently poetical to encourage the lad to give utterance to the expressions of devotion that he had composed the previous evening; he was forced to fall back on something less high flown:

"Do you know I wanted to write to you from Turin — indeed I did write several times."

"Good Heavens! but no letters ever reached me!" exclaimed Rachel, terrified at the notion of those effusions in the hands of heaven knows who.

"Do not be uneasy," Giovanni hastened to add. "I wrote, but I did not send the letters."

"Then why did you write them?"

"Because I felt that I must — I had so much to say to you." Then after a short pause he went on, lowering his voice: "And you — did you never feel so?"

"You ask too much," said Rachel with a blush — a blush which meant yes, that she too had written, that she was a little ashamed of it, but that she longed to give him those suppressed documents and to read his.

Giovanni had to a great extent conquered his

schoolboy bashfulness; he dared to look his
pretty neighbor straight in the eyes, and he did
not blush; she, on her part, ventured to glance at
him from time to time, and the oftener when they
happened to be at some little distance apart; and
they said all sorts of tender things with their melancholy gaze; words could not have been more
eloquent, they understood each other now; in
their mute dialogue each said to the other: "If
only we were alone!"

Every evening Rachel went to walk or sit on
the terrace at the bottom of the garden and Giovanni would pass up and down the road on the
further side of the moat with his eyes fixed on her;
while she gazed after him as long as he was in
sight; and he would turn round at every step,
linger to look back, and at last, at the bend in the
road, when he had passed and repassed till it was
quite dark and they could hardly see each other, he
would take off his hat very slowly, so as to pro-
long the bow to which she responded with a slight
sign of recognition. The possibilities of that twilight meeting formed the subject of their waking
dreams all day. After the first time, they had each,
without any agreement, returned at the same hour,

she to the terrace, and he to the road below; and
the same performance always was repeated — he
walked up and down, they gazed and bowed at
parting; but it was an exquisite joy, and they
were both wretched when by some accident one
or the other failed to keep the unspoken tryst.
The day after such an absence the defaulter put
on every demonstration of guilt and penitence and
the other, who had been punctual, gave signs of
indignation. In short, by dint of glances — which,
however, at such a distance had no more expression than a stare — they succeeded in agitating
each other in turns, in feeling rapture or misery,
and in stirring up that tempest of emotions which
makes young hearts beat wildly and leaves them
passive victims of admiration, love, and longing.

CHAPTER XII.

THE feast of St. Alexander was over; and was even ceasing to be the sole theme of conversation; every one who happened to have a plot of vines on the sunny slope of the hill was beginning to think of the vintage. The Dottorino did not own a single leaf or stem in all the vegetable kingdom; the carnation that bloomed on the window ledge in a broken bowl was La Matta's property, and the bowl even had been only hypothetically his, since he had never paid for it. But the doctor was no less the soul of the vintage than he was of the dinner-table.

"You may trust me to eat none of your grapes," he said. "The fox who only discovered that those grapes were sour that were out of reach was not half so acute as I am. He did not know that even those in the basket are always sour. Graves are never ripe enough for me till they have been through the wine-vat." And of course the proprietors did not fail to produce a bottle of the ripe grape and taste it with him; they knew too well its happy effects on the doctor's jolly soul to withhold this encouragement.

One day Giovanni and his father happened to meet on the high-road and the doctor proposed that his son should accompany him to Signor Pedrotti's vineyard where they were about to pull the white grapes, spending the day there. Rachel would not go out on the terrace that evening then. Giovanni felt a sudden deference to the paternal desire. . . He only turned round and walked by his side till they reached the vineyard, it is true, then they parted and took different paths, the old man making at once by the shortest way to the lodge in the grounds. All the rank and fashion of Fontanetto were present and Giovanni could catch fragments of conversations through the vines.

"They are as sweet as honey," said the secretary's grim-visaged wife in the tone in which she might have said: "They are poison."

"I always want the bunches that are out of reach," said a young shrill voice.

"Then there is one that will make your mouth water," remarked Rachel, stooping down and thrusting one arm as far as she could stretch through the branches that trailed over the ground, while she supported herself with the other on the burnt chalky earth. But the bunch was far, far in —quite on the further side of the vine-row and she could not gather it. She felt something hot touch her hand and some one grasped it for an instant; when she drew it back she saw that she held a carnation.

"What is the matter? What made you cry out?" asked her companion.

"I scratched myself among the branches," replied Rachel who had recognized the burning lips and the carnation as those of Giovanni.

Then, as she moved on, looking for the best bunches of grapes, she gradually increased her pace till, stooping once more, she disappeared under the trailing boughs of the vines and was lost among them. There was nothing to hinder her; in a vineyard everyone goes where he pleases. She had acted without any distinct plan; she only knew that Giovanni was there and her heart prompted her to escape from the crowd. In a moment he had caught sight of her pretty head through the vines, crowned with leaves like a young Bacchus. He gazed at her with eager and

melancholy eyes, and his fixed gaze attracted her
irresistibly.   With her head bent, her cheeks scarlet and with a slow reluctant step, she walked towards him as though in a mesmeric trance; he
bowed low and lifting the branches that were in
her way made an arch under which she passed in
silence.   The boughs fell again, and the pair stood
face to face; pale now, tremulous and palpitating,
alone in the alley between the vine rows, where
the grapes had all been plucked.   Giovanni took
her hand and said:

"I am going the day after to-morrow — then,
for a year, we shall not meet again."

Rachel bent her head but she said nothing.
Giovanni's tall figure was very close to hers, and
his face, bending above her head, tingled with a
vehement longing to clasp her in his arms; his
warm breath fanned the tendrils of her wreath
and she felt it on her ear and throat.   Rachel
sighed deeply, as if she had some great trouble on
her mind.   He too sighed; and then, as though
to give some relief to the oppression that weighed
on them both, he drew her arm through his own
as if she were his wife, but without leaving go of
her hand.

"You are mine — always mine?" he asked in a whisper.

"Yes, yes," replied Rachel with another sigh, and then she added: "We will be like a brother and sister."

It was a phrase she had picked up from some novel. To Giovanni it was the most delicious evidence of childlike innocence; a strain of heavenly poetry. He felt that he ought to go down on his knees to her for that speech, and he promised her that he would indeed always love her so. At that moment he really believed himself capable of such sublime heights. After this they found no more to say; they walked on in silence both very grave and both much troubled in soul; pressing each other's hands to gain courage, and as serious and mute as though they had performed some solemn rite. When they reached the end of the alley they separated. They had clung closely together until then, but now, at the moment when he bent down to kiss her, Giovanni was suddenly conscious of the open sky, and the wide world around them, he drew her aside under a cherry tree from which the despoiled branches of a vine hung in festoons. There, under the green vault, hidden from the world and the all-seeing sky, he spread his arms with a beseeching gesture; he wanted Rachel to nestle in them of her own free will. She flew to his heart, and he clasped her with a vehemence that gave the lie to their fraternal projects; but their souls were innocent; and the Cherubim and Seraphim, the Thrones and Dominions — nay the eleven thousand virgins themselves, might have looked down on that passionate and desperate embrace without a blush.

When the doctor and his son came home from the vineyard La Matta was diligently watering and weeding her carnation. She had counted its flowers again and again; and she was sure that one was missing. That morning Giovanni had gone out for his walk with a carnation in his button-hole and La Matta was singing and laughing with all her heart and watered her plant with more satisfaction than ever, and counted its flowers once more. When Giovanni came in the .girl went out to meet him with a broad smile on her face; but the next instant she had ceased to smile and went back to her kitchen — the carnation was gone.

Later in the evening the Dottorino was standing at his front door; all the party who had remained to dine up at Pedrotti's vineyard were coming home down the hill and when they reached the doctor's house they paused to say good evening. La Matta was at the window again, but she was not singing now. She looked down on the Signorina Pedrotti, and seeing how tall and handsome she was, and how well dressed, she reflected with stupid satisfaction: "She cannot play with Giovanni now-a-days."

At this moment Giovanni himself stepped out on the balcony of his room, calling out: "Good evening." "Good evening," answered one and another, and then, after the rest, Rachel's voice, clear, but somewhat tremulous, said: "Good evening," and she glanced up at Giovanni and smelt at a carnation.

Next morning, when Giovanni went to the window to gather another carnation, he found nothing, not even the cracked bowl. La Matta never would understand his enquiries nor tell him what had become of the carnation plant. She only shrugged her shoulders and said: "I do not know." But, in fact, Giovanni hardly dared

to question her very closely, La Matta was
so excessively cross during those few days.
She eat nothing and her eyes were always red
with crying. Some one was ill, perhaps, at her
foster-mother's.

CHAPTER XIII.

YEARS went by. Giovanni proved indeed that his talents were exceptional; he studied indefatigably, spoke well, wrote elegantly, and was not a bad poet. As he grew older and learnt more, his love too throve and grew, and was a serious motive in his life. As the lad became a man and knew more of the world, his judgment ripened, and his passion, while it was less romantic, was deeper and truer. The fraternal relations he had accepted in a moment of youthful aberration now made him smile. He had returned to Fontanetto every autumn, but now that he was a man—and, indeed, for that very reason — he never found himself alone with Rachel. Nevertheless they felt themselves bound to each other just as much as though they had been betrothed. Their eyes, which never failed to meet as though an electric current flashed between them, their hands, which clasped and clung so eagerly, held them as securely as a pledge in words could have done. They had long

memories of their patient and romantic love and
it had all been like this — speechless.

Even Signor Pedrotti was effusive about Giovanni and appeared to be very fond of him; indeed, when his college life was over and Giovanni
came home loaded with laurels, he was so affectionate to him that the lad grew quite confident.
It was evident that there was nothing he would
like better than to call him his son.   Now it was
the eve of Giovanni's departure for Milan where
he was about to enter on his career as a lawyer.
He had eaten his last dinner at the castle and
matters were just where they had so long been ;
but Signor Pedrotti had that evening been particularly friendly to his protégé; he had embraced
him repeatedly, speaking of him as : " our young
avvocato."

" You are now launched on a splendid career,"
he had said. " You are not to disappoint me you
know.   Remember that I have promised myself
that I shall see you a great man.   I have put my
faith in you, and now that you have won your
laurels it lies with you to do me credit."

Then he had embraced him once more and
added :   " Who knows whether we may not see

you deputy some day and have to apply to you
for all that concerns the welfare of our part of the
country? Who knows I say — if only you are
determined . . . Where there's a will there's a
way."

All this was said with an air of thorough good
faith, but his real motive was rather to remind
Giovanni of the share he had had in planting that
crop of laurels and to patronize the young man,
than genuine admiration.

Giovanni however took it all for gospel. " I
put my faith in you — where there's a will there's
a way." He had the will to win Rachel; and if
her father had faith in his talents, why should
there not be a way too? And Rachel herself perhaps thought the same for she smiled as she saw
her father so affectionate in his demeanor towards
her lover. Presently, as Rachel handed him his
coffee cup, Giovanni whispered: " I must speak
to you before I leave."

" Speak," she said standing for a moment as if
to hand him the sugar.

" No, no; alone!" She did not seem at all
angry, but looked at him doubtfully, as much as
to say it was impossible.

"It is dark," she murmured, "we cannot go
out in the garden."

"No, not now, but to-morrow — if you will go
out on the terrace I will cross the river by the
bridge where the water is low and under the
wall. . ."

He could think of no way of raising himself to
a level that would make him worthy of Signor
Pedrotti's daughter but by quitting his home and
her, and working long and bravely in one of the
great cities of Italy ; but he dreaded lest, during
his absence, while he was only laying the foundations of their future, another suitor — a rich proprietor perhaps—should come to ask Rachel's hand
and carry her off. This thought chilled his soul
and damped his courage. He felt that he must
drag it out of his heart like a thorn. He there-
fore made up his mind first to claim a solemn
promise from Rachel, and then prefer his suit to
her father and carry her pledge with him as a
talisman.

The next day Rachel had a headache and preferred sitting in the air quietly on the terrace
while her father went with some friends up to the
vineyard, where the leaves were now all fallen and

the vines no longer offered any retreat for lovers; where the must was already fermenting in the vats, and the masters found nothing to do but to play a game of bésique in the deserted lodge with all the windows shut. Giovanni made his way across the little bridge and under the terrace wall where he was half hidden by the brambles that grew over the bank. Rachel leaned over the parapet, looking as pale and worn as though she really had a bad headache. It was the same quiet hour, the air was as damp and still, the autumn shadows as softly gloomy, as on a similar occasion three years before; but in those three years their spirits had developed and ripened; Giovanni was a lawyer and two and twenty. There was no hesitation now, no seeking for words and phrases; they spoke with the ready flow of love and mutual confidence. They could not even reach to take hands, but he looked up at her with ardent eyes, and he said to her in his enchanting voice:

"Listen, Rachel; I want you to give up loving me as a brother. We are no longer two simple children; you know — you must feel — that such love as that is not what I want of you."

"No, yes, I know," sighed Rachel, bashful and

blushing, but utterly sincere. He gazed into her eyes, putting into that gaze all the passion that he would fain have put into a kiss if only he could have reached her; then he went on :

" Will you allow me to ask your father to promise you to me before I go ?"

" Oh yes, yes!" whispered Rachel tenderly. Giovanni went on as if he were talking to himself rather than to her, perfectly happy at receiving this consent which so fully assured him of her love :

" I hope, my darling, that you may never have reason to repent of your words. You will see that this is not a mere boyish fancy on my part. I am confident that I shall make myself a name and a position worthy of you. You cannot know — no one can think, what strength and courage your love has given me. If I ever do anything worth doing I shall owe it all to you, for it was the thought of you that spurred me to a noble ambition; to hard work and high aims; and to win you I hope and intend to conquer a place in the world, and earn wealth."

He spoke humbly but with such a ring of passion in his voice that Rachel's heart thrilled as she

listened. She answered only with those ardent
eyes of hers and he went on:

"Do you think that I should ever have worked,
that I should at this moment have taken my degree, if it had not been for you? I have the seeds
of every evil passion in my soul, and at Turin
there are temptations enough to debase any man.
If I had not fed on that one desire that has absorbed all my being I should have taken life lightly
enough, have wasted all my best years, have disgusted your father and the others, and have come
back here to mind sheep, as my father used to say;
or have sunk to the level of those degraded creatures who swarm in great cities, alternating between
misery and vice. It is you who have saved me
and spurred me to good issues and you still must
be my guardian spirit, standing as the prize and
goal of all my efforts, as the reward, the hope, the
delight and the repose of my life."

He threw up his hands as if beseeching her to
clasp them across the space that divided them;
she leaned over and stretched down, but they
could not join. A terrible discouragement came
over her lover as he saw how fatally they were
parted.

" And if after all," he exclaimed, " your father refuses me ?"

" For pity's sake do not think of such a thing!" she cried. " It would be dreadful."

" But if he did, tell me, what would you do ?"

" I should die," she whispered.

" No, no, that is mere romance," answered Giovanni impatiently. " Besides I will not have you die ; you must live and be mine at all costs. You will — say that you will."

" Yes."

" Even if your father forbids it."

" That would be impossible."   ·

" Why ?"

" Why . . . because . . . I do not know ; but I could not disobey my father. I have always done as he wished, and he has always been so kind to me. . ." Then as if to drive away such dismal thoughts she added : " But we will not think of anything so miserable. He is so affectionate to you ; and to-day he said he had put his faith in you. What makes you fancy he can refuse you ?"

" To be sure," replied Giovanni, " we will not forecast evil." Then making an ineffectual attempt to scale the wall he asked her : " You love me ?"

She held her fingers to her lips and shed the kiss
upon him, as it were, not smiling but gravely, with
the deep emotion with which we seal some solemn
act.

Giovanni pulled himself so far up the wall as
to reach the tip of her toes that peeped through
the spaces between the balustrades, and with his
free hand he clasped her foot and kissed the
fingers that had touched it.

The plain below floated in a sea of mist; even
the white line of the high-road was scarcely visible on the other side of the moat; but through
the fog, backwards and forwards, they could distinguish a figure which stood still from time to
time opposite Rachel, looking first at her and then
down into the water.

" Good-bye," murmured Rachel, " I must be
going.   Some one is watching us."

" Oh never mind her ; it is La Matta."

CHAPTER XIV.

GIOVANNI spent the night in arranging everything for his departure. He was not going back
to the college so he was to have an allowance no
longer from his patrons. He was going to the
office of a famous lawyer in Milan, where he would
first learn his business and then take work in the
courts; he had no fears for the future; his life at
school and at college had been a succession of
triumphs; the position of Berti, the great man
under whom he was about to enter life, would
smooth his way; and love was jubilant in his
heart.

The doctor came in late that evening; he had
been drinking with one and another and was in
capital spirits. As he passed by the kitchen door
he fancied that he saw, sitting on the hearthstone
where the fire was out, a crouching creature rocking
itself and wailing. " It must be the cat," thought
the doctor, whose sense of proportion was somewhat obscured, and he went his way. But it was

not the cat; the crouching figure on the hearth never stirred till morning.

Giovanni sang a love song as he dressed; his fine tenor notes had never sounded clearer or richer. He was still singing as he went down-stairs and out into the road; in the silence of the early day the solitary voice was heard till it died away in the distance. He wandered along the foot-paths that zigzagged up the hills, still singing, spouting poetry, building castles in the air — interrupting himself, beginning again from the foundations — anxious and impatient. Finally, at ten o'clock, he went to the castle and asked to speak to the master. But the mere sight of the servant who showed him in quelled his confidence. He crossed the deserted dining-room, and the great dusty sideboards, the piles of china, the cupboards full of plate, depressed him deeply. What a gulf, good heaven! between all this splendor and his destitution! Then they went through a large drawing-room with the blinds down and the shutters closed; and the huge sofas in the holland covers with their obese and puffy cushions, looked to his fancy in the dim light like a party of corpulent county magnates gravely waiting till he should have preferred his petition to discuss it among themselves. At length he reached Signor Pedrotti's study, which looked cold and stern in its nakedness. There were a few chairs and a writing-table; but on each side of this table stood a set of shelves with an endless array of deed boxes, and on each box was written in large Roman type the name of an estate. Signor Pedrotti was writing in a ledger; he looked up for a moment and said:

"Ah, you are off then? Wait a moment till I have finished this note."

Giovanni's courage had entirely oozed out; he felt his heart beating now that the time had come for facing the great question. He stood mechanically reading the names of the deed boxes: *Il Gentilino, la Peveraccia, Sant' Antonio al Fosso* . . . They were but small properties, still they were properties; he knew them all well, but he knew nothing of their value; he counted the boxes — there were fourteen and they were to him as fourteen enemies standing there to convict him of his indigence. Signor Pedrotti closed his ledger and looked up, saying, as he turned to Giovanni:

" Then you are off, my boy ?"

" Yes — to start on my career," replied Giovanni.

" And you have come to take leave ?" asked
the elder, for the sake of saying something.

" Yes. . ."

" Have you been to say good-bye to the Count
Valle, and to the vicar ?"

" No, I came first to you."

" That is well, thank you. Will you stay to
breakfast ? Then you can say good-bye to
Rachel."

Giovanni felt himself turn cold. His hands
were like ice, and damp with chill dews, and his
heart leaped so violently that his breath came
short and his voice shook. Still, his patron's
friendly tone was encouraging, and fully resolved
to speak, he said : •

" No, thank you. I came in fact to speak to
you . . . about a matter of great importance . . .
to me. . ."

" Speak out; if I can do anything," answered
his host with a patronizing air. Then, seeing that
he was timid, he added : " Do not be afraid ; your
future is secured ; you have excellent capabilities

and you are beginning under a capital man. Work, keep up your courage, and you will see; you know that I have always believed in you. The world is for the young, my dear boy."

"Yes — but the old — that is to say those who are a little older — must help them a little."

"They have helped you as it seems to me," said Pedrotti, taking umbrage at the luckless epithet old, and at the idea that Giovanni did not duly appreciate his past favors and was about to ask for more.

"Yes, and whatever I am I owe to you," said Giovanni, more and more nervously. "But you know we all have our dreams and aspirations — I want to achieve something further."

"That is very right. Ambition is what makes great men and great deeds," said Pedrotti sentcn-tiously, quoting from his newspaper.

"Indeed, it makes me very happy to hear you say so; for I have an ambition — a great ambition," stammered Giovanni, who could no longer control his beating heart or his quavering voice.

"Well and good, and may I be informed of what this great ambition is?" 'asked the lord of

the castle very graciously.   "Do you want to sit
in parliament?"

"No — I want — to marry your daughter,"
whispered Giovanni almost inaudibly.

Signor Pedrotti sat bolt upright; he fixed a
stony eye on the young man and for a few minutes
was absolutely speechless.   Then he repeated, as
though he was not sure that he had heard :

"Marry my daughter!"

Giovanni bowed as a guilty culprit might, and
proffered his best argument from the very bottom
of his heart :

"I love her so. . ."

"You. do me too much honor," said Signor
Pedrotti sarcastically.

"And she loves me," said Giovanni, in whom
indignation had almost revived his courage.

"I am delighted to hear it—but do you know
what my daughter's fortune will be?"

"I have not asked her and I would marry her
if she had no more than I have myself."

"Oh, very good, then we will discuss the subject another time."   And the worthy gentleman
rose as much as to put an end to the interview.

But Giovanni had recovered his presence of mind under this discourteous refusal and he persisted.

"I shall be quite satisfied if you will promise not to make her marry any one else, and promise me that I may win her when I have made a name and a fortune."

"Oh, I cannot discount bills that do not fall due for so long," said Pedrotti with a shrug and moving towards the door.

"Did you not say that you had faith in me?" asked Giovanni in reproachful accents.

"We have had enough of this!" exclaimed Pedrotti, stamping with rage. • "I have listened to you too long already. Do you suppose that because you have won that sprig of bays that we have paid for you are a made man? My daughter is not for you — neither now nor at any time; get that well into your head. I mean her to marry some one worthy of her and of me."

"But I might become worthy of her," urged Giovanni quivering with indignation.

"Merciful Heaven!" interrupted the elder, flinging his words in Giovanni's face like a blow. "Merciful Heaven! the Dottorino's son worthy of my daughter! Never! — Be off with you, and never let me see you anywhere near my house again.   Good God !"

And he shut the door himself on the unhappy lover with a slam that was more eloquent than words.   .

CHAPTER XV.

GIOVANNI almost flew across the fields, home ; his face was flushed and his nerves all jarring with rage.   He rushed up into his own room, and slammed his door with a vehement bang, as though he, in his turn, were slamming it in the face of the rich man who had scorned him.   Then he sat down to write to Rachel :

"Your father is a wretch, a heartless wretch ;" and he went on to relate in hot wrath, all the interview with the lord of the castle, with no end of "I said to him," "and then he replied." However, when he had written a few sentences, and paused to recollect the exact order of the dialogue, it struck him that he was putting himself in the wrong by thus abusing the father in writing to the daughter; he felt that it was beneath him, and began again, uttering what in fact lay nearer to his heart.

" We were far too hopeful yesterday evening; we shut our eyes to the possibility of evil, and the evil has fallen upon us and found us unprepared. Your father has refused the promise I entreated of him, and has shut me out of his house forever.

" I am deeply hurt; if, nevertheless, I may fix my hopes on you I shall not be crushed. I shall feel quite capable of proving that talents are a match for wealth. But you said one dreadful thing yesterday — you said that you could not resist your father's will. Will you obey him then ? Will you reject me, to marry some rich man, some landowner, or fund-holder ? I have no heart to think of it. I hope for — I ask — I claim your promise to be mine and to wait for me. It is a bold request, and the promise on your part will be no light matter; think of it seriously. Much and desperately as I love you, I could not bear to cheat you of your pledge under an illusion. The day of fulfilment must be a distant one, you will have to wait for years; but I feel that I have the energy and capacity to make a brilliant position. Still, I must have something more than a name and a good income before I can again face your father after all he has said to me; I must have funded capital to lay in the other scale, and balance that detested fortune that he is to give you; and such a capital is slow in accumulating.

" It must be long, perhaps very long, before I can claim the fulfilment of that tender promise; and meanwhile we must live apart and no one will ever mention my name even, in your hearing. Your father will urge the claims of other suitors dearer to his fancy, and you will have to reject them—not without a struggle, while he will guess the reason of your refusal, and there may be scenes of strife that will embitter your life. It is much, too much, to ask of a weak woman's heart; and even as I ask this utmost favor in the name of love — of our love — I hardly dare hope that you will grant it.

" Still, if you feel that you are strong enough for such a sacrifice write one word, simply '*yes*,' and slip it into the volume of *I Promessi Sposi* that I lent you and which I will desire La Matta to fetch, as an excuse for sending her to your house, where I should have the door shut upon me.

"Oh Rachel! if I should find that line in your writing I will bless you from the bottom of my soul; and it will give me such courage, such energy, that I shall feel myself master of the world. I will spend every hour, every minute of my life in toil, in the hope of making you some return for your disinterested sacrifice, and when I have won you I will devote my leisure to worshipping you.

"But in truth I dare not hope it. You are a woman, and young. Your father loves you truly, and it becomes you to obey him. It is your duty, and I know it, my darling. The little book will come back to me without bringing me any such joy. But I shall still feel that you love me, that you are suffering — grieving, but resigned, and that you have abandoned me to my fate. It will be a terrible blow and will leave a deep wound — but indeed I love you so that I shall forgive you."

When he had sealed this letter he went in search of La Matta. He found her in the kitchen, huddled on the hearth and rocking herself dolefully.

He roused her and said, very distinctly, that she might not misunderstand him :

" Go up to the castle, and say that I have sent you to ask for a book that I lent to the signorina."

La Matta sat stolidly sulky, with her head down, as if she did not intend to stir.

" Do you understand ?" asked Giovanni.

She gave a wriggle : " I do not know," she muttered.

But Giovanni was in no mood to be patient, and he went on in an angry tone :

" But it is absolutely necessary that you should do this errand. Repeat what I say : ' Signor Giovanni has sent me. . .''

La Matta looked him hard in the face ; she saw that he was pale, agitated and trembling; and she repeated her lesson with all the attention of which she was capable. When she had said it Giovanni went on, giving her his letter :

" When you are shown in to the signorina and there is no one by to see, give her this letter ; but mind that no one sees it."

La Matta took the letter doubtfully, and set out slowly and unwillingly.

"Make haste!" Giovanni cried after her, "for Heaven's sake hurry!"

For a minute or two she mended her pace; but no sooner had she turned the corner than she stopped, took the letter out of her pocket, turned it over and examined it closely, trying to read the address—but the only letter she could recognize was the O, so she pocketed it again with a sigh and slowly made her way to the house. Giovanni meanwhile was counting the minutes, and fuming with impatience; at length, utterly incapable of controlling himself, he set out to meet the girl as she returned. He saw her loitering on her way back along the edge of the castle moat, with her head sunk and a heavy step. She no sooner caught sight of him than she turned round as if she wanted to escape; but he overtook her, and seized the book.

"No, no, I will carry it," said the girl. But Giovanni would not yield. She put out her hand to snatch it back; she was trembling and seemed frightened.

"Why should you carry it?" she said. "It is my place to carry it."

Giovanni however kept possession of it, and ran home clutching the volume with both hands.

When he reached his room he anxiously opened
it — it contained nothing — he shook it — nothing
fell out.   Pale, gasping, and with trembling hands,
he turned over all the leaves one by one — he
found nothing.

"I knew it!" he groaned.   "She told me that
she could not resist her father."   And then he
added:

"She too! — Well she will see! . . ."

He went out and hastily paid his calls; taking
leave of his patrons, with abrupt audacity, talking
excitedly of his future prospects and certain success.   There was a defiance in his manner which
to these worthy folks seemed very strange.

"So much the better, my boy, go on and
prosper," they said.   "If you make a fortune so
much the better for you.   I only hope you
may."

But when his back was turned they shook their
heads: "What has come over him?   He seems
as if he had been drinking."

Giovanni went home in a carriage he had hired
to carry him to the railway station at Borgomanero.   On going into his room to fetch his
luggage he discovered La Matta, who was once

more examining the volume she had brought back from the castle.

"Let that alone," he exclaimed angrily; and snatching it out of her hand he flung the precious second edition of *I Promessi Sposi* on to the top shelf of the bookcase. Then he took a hasty leave of his father, got into the vehicle and was gone.

"She too!—Well she will see!" he muttered once more as the crazy conveyance carried him past the castle moat. Either Rachel had been convinced by her father's vulgar arguments, or she had submitted, though unconvinced, to the weight of his authority. In either case she did not love him with such passion as he had hoped; she had not perfect faith in him. His soul was filled with bitterness at the thought, but his courage was not quenched; on the contrary, it spurred him to work harder than ever to conquer a position in society that he might be able to say to her: "You see, you were wrong to distrust me."

He had thought that he needed her promise to keep up his resolution, but now the very lack of that promise gave force to his will because it made him fear that success would come too late. He must make haste to be rich and famous as soon as possible, while Rachel was still young, and before anyone else should marry her.

The idea seethed in his blood like a fever. To his heated fancy the long future and the flying present were but one; he felt as though he must always run, fly, hasten, never lose an instant; as though he were starting on a race with some imaginary rival. The jog-trot of the sorry beast that dragged him to Borgomanero made him writhe with impatience; when he had started in the train the engine seemed as slow as the horse. He could not sit still; he opened and shut the window, looked at his watch, and at the time-table, counted the stations, calculated the minutes the train was late, and when they reached Novara complained to the porter that they were ninety-five seconds behind time. Those two minutes were lost out of his future.

CHAPTER XVI.

THE early days of Giovanni's residence at Milan were like a pail of cold water on his ardor. Signor Pedrotti, in recommending the poor boy to the avvocato Berti a month before, had written :

"Remember that he has nothing but what he may be able to earn in your office; kindly try to find him as cheap a lodging as possible, with such board as is within the means of an indigent lad as he is."

The lawyer paid him a salary of fifty francs a month, and he had taken a room quite close to the office from a maker of wooden clogs and lasts. It was not a room properly speaking; indeed, only two years since it had been part of the shop. Then the last-maker had married and he had cut his shop in two horizontally, setting up the conjugal couch in the upper room thus obtained. Then the wife, who was of an economical turn, had thought it possible to divide off a portion of this mezzanine apartment and make two of it. Thus, out of a single shop, they had ended by making a shop and two bedrooms. The first cabin, however, was only a sort of open loft into which you put your head through a large hole in the floor as you mounted the spiral stairs that led up to it. This had not prevented the owners from putting up a bed against one wall, and a rickety table against the other, which, with two chairs, constituted a *furnished apartment* that they let at twelve francs a month. Notwithstanding the paucity of furniture the room was not empty. The walls and ceiling were lined with huge bunches of lasts and sabots, tied together by the heels so that they stuck out in every direction like the spines on a burr. All round the arch of the shop window which gave light to the upper floor, on each side of the stairs, and from the opening into the loft, hung these feet innumerable, of all shapes and sizes; you had to mount carefully for fear of hurting your head and take every precaution with a lighted candle.

This was the lodging assigned to Giovanni; but he was not fastidious. " It is cheap," he said,

" and at that price I can hardly expect to get any better. . ." and the mistress of the establishment, encouraged by his easy resignation, ventured to say: " If you like to arrange to take your share of our soup. . ."

" What are you thinking of?" interrupted her husband.

" Never you mind, I say it as much for his advantage as ours. It will not cost him much and after all, if he does not like it. . ."

Giovanni agreed at thirty centesimi a day, which was to include a share in a bottle of wine ; but he soon discovered that for his young appetite this meal was no more than a luncheon ; leaving him in fact very ready for the next; so he had found an eating-house where he could dine at thirty francs a month. Thus his monthly salary was fully disposed of—indeed one franc more, and to supply that one and the cost of washing, lights, relaxation, clothes, boots and everything else that he might want, the young lawyer must earn something. His master would give him law-deeds to copy and notes of cases to arrange ; and now and then he had some clause of an English or German book to translate. By these means Giovanni

managed to cke out his monthly allowance, but
Berti kept him busy in the office all day; he had
only the early morning and the evening for the
work that was to bring him this small extra pay,
and little as he slept the twenty-four hours of the
day were never too many for him.

His room had neither chimney nor stove; the
ill-joined flooring admitted all the cold air from
the shop where the door was incessantly opening
and shutting, and the walls sweated with damp.
The last-maker said that it was best so as there was
the less danger that his stock would catch fire. But
this reflection did not save Giovanni from having
his limbs stiff and his hands numb with cold during
the long winter evenings that he spent there in
solitude, writing by the light of a petroleum lamp.
This lamp was the cause of endless squabbles
with his landlord. No sooner had his big, round
head—with its fringe of hair, but bald in the middle, like that of St. Joseph — made its appearance
above the floor, rising as he came up the stairs,
then a series of loud sniffs were audible following
up the scent, then a succession of grunts and, at
last, while his heavy tread shook the beams, he
could be heard muttering: " That confounded

petroleum.   And with such a lot of wood about!
dear me ! dear me !"

Giovanni would go on writing, but the grumbling was continued on the other side of the par-
tition, between his hosts, who, by reason of the
thinness of the wall had no secrets from their
lodger.   But they were not bad folks, and the
young law student went his own way and let them
talk.   Sometimes when the cold was most intense,
as he heard this worthy couple tucking themselves
into their bed of maize husks, and calling up fear-
ful visions of conflagrations, he felt an insane desire to build up a pile of lasts and sabots and
chips, and set fire to them and warm himself at
the blaze.   But then he would think of Rachel
and say to himself: " Some day she will know
what I have endured for her sake."   And he took
a pride in these discomforts and he felt himself a
hero.

Thus in the secrecy of his own room he could
glory in his poverty.   But out of it he often suffered keen humiliation.   On his first arrival in the
office the other clerks had given him to understand
that it was the custom to do honor to a new-comer
by giving him a dinner and that he would be ex-

pected to give them a dinner in return. Giovanni had let the subject drop; but the senior clerk, who knew what the circumstances of a poor student were likely to be, had added to encourage him: "These are not the banquets of Lucullus you know. Dinners at five francs a head."

Still, there were four of them, and twenty francs was a sum quite beyond Giovanni's resources. For some little time nothing more was said, and he thought to himself, at once comforted and mortified, "they understand how it is." They had understood very well, and about three weeks after the eldest of the party said to Giovanni, in the name of the others who were both present:

"I say, we have agreed to invite you to come and dine with us to-morrow to celebrate your joining us; it is only the usual thing,—if you will give us the pleasure. . ."

Giovanni felt very uncomfortable and turned very red; he felt that he ought to have thanked them and have said at once that he hoped on such a day to have the pleasure of seeing them to dine with him. But then he remembered how few his coins were and that he had no credit, and the impossibility of the situation choked the words in his throat. Then the senior clerk, who was a good-hearted fellow, added :

" You are not expected to return it you know. No ceremony. . ."

It was a blow, and Giovanni felt it. That evening his poverty was a real grievance ; he could have fought with fate as he went into the shop. The shavings that crunched under his step irritated him beyond bearing ; he kicked them out of his way and made straight for the stairs, paying no heed to the festoons of lasts and clogs that hung in every direction. The first clump of lasts that hit him in the side he struck out at violently.

" Look out there !" the man called up from the shop.

But Giovanni was at the end of his patience. He gave himself an angry shake and stalked up the narrow stairs in a rage, pushing aside every impediment with his fists. As he reached the top he hit his head against an enormous bunch of sabots which fell off the nail, rolling and clattering with as much noise as a cart-load of stones and gravel. The last-maker and his wife started to their feet exclaiming loudly, and all the evening there came up from the shop, with the noise of the

plane and the adze, the angry vituperations of the
scandalized couple. Late at night, when Giovanni
who could not fix his mind on his work, had retired to meditate on his mortification in bed, he
saw them go through his room to their own, carrying the clump of wooden shoes like a wounded
sufferer whom common pity required them to
place in safer quarters out of the way of a dan-
gerous foe, at whom they cast indignant glances.
From that time his life was increasingly comfort-
less; no one in the house ever spoke a word to
him. He eat his breakfast in silence while the
last-maker's wife bustled about the shop sweeping
and dusting, and her husband every now and then
would observe satirically :

"Take care you do not sweep the chips under
the young gentleman's feet; and wait to dust till
he is out of the way, you might make him dusty."
And in the evening, when Giovanni was going
upstairs, the man would march up in front of him
with his arms outspread, pushing aside the
bunches of wooden shoes in a mockery of politeness.

At the office, on the other hand, he never felt
easy on account of that dinner that he had not

been able to return. It stood like a shadow
between him and the other clerks, and checked
their equality of intimacy. There were a whole
series of subjects that he felt he dared not approach
lest they should suggest the topic that always
made him blush. They could not discuss dining-
houses, nor dinners, nor invitations; and if one of
his comrades only said to another: "Shall we
dine together to-day?" he felt it as an ironical
hint and was nettled by it.

It happened one day that the other clerks had
arranged to dine in a party in honor of the birthday of one of them and they discussed it in an
undertone that he might not hear them; but this,
which they meant kindly, he felt as an insult, and
he determined to return the banquet he had accepted at any cost. He gave up wine at his daily
dinner, and worked later at night, and at the end
of two months found himself rich enough to give
the all-important invitation on the strength of
twenty-five francs that he had scraped together
and hoarded up, sou by sou. He had calculated
that he could not be sure of spending less, with
the fee to the waiter, coffee, cigars, and other certain expenses, not to mention the dreadful un-

foreseen extras. They were twenty-five drops of his heart's blood. But as he came out of the eating-house followed by his three companions, his head a little heavy.from a glass of wine more than usual, and his purse the lighter by those five and twenty francs, he felt that he had recovered caste, and as his thoughts turned to Rachel he reflected: "I must be able to tell her that even in my hardest straits I never stooped to meanness." And the sense of having deserved her good opinion did more to make up to him for the privations he had suffered than the vain satisfaction of having returned the dinner.

CHAPTER XVII.

THERE were particular seasons when Giovanni's poverty brought him many bitter stings. One of these was the carnival, and particularly the last week of that festive season. Then his fellow-clerks would chatter and whisper all day of the amusements of the evening; fitful snatches of talk with

allusions and suggestions that Giovanni had difficulty in piecing out.

"Which did you admire most last evening, the
dark girl or that fair one ? She was a real beauty.
What a color! and what a dress! She puts some
money on her back !"

Giovanni would scribble as fast as he could,
making his pen scratch and squeak that he might
not hear; but the words would get mixed up with
the legal phraseology that he copied on to the
paper, and filled his brain with dreams, wishes,
and intense curiosity. His one idea was to get
out and forget these fancies; but then, when he
was out of doors, it was worse; the streets were
crowded with a gay and noisy rabble; everybody
in the town seemed to have money to spend, the
poorest workmen were free with their cash and
giving themselves a good time. The city was like
an ants' nest of peddlers and itinerant sellers of
prints, caricatures, paper flowers, cockades, medals,
and all the grotesque absurdities of the carnival.
But they did not offer their wares to Giovanni,
they only grinned at him ironically, as much as to
say: "He's no good — he's cleaned out." The
eating-shops displayed their most tempting wares

—fat geese, and fair and corpulent capons exposed
their portly persons by the side of melancholy
cray-fish which now and then moved a claw in a
languid dying effort. The sausages assumed
gigantic proportions, and the windows were full of
rich cheeses, truffles, shining fish, and bottles of
rare vintages, proving how surely the vendors
could reckon on the gluttony or the generosity of
holiday customers. From every tavern and eating-
house proceeded a constant clatter of plates, and
a tuneless jingle of glasses and spoons; while from
the kitchen below rose the steamy odors of roast
and boiled irresistibly suggesting to Giovanni visions of a warm room and of a neatly laid table,
brightly lighted and secure from draughts, where
he should be snugly shut in to enjoy a good dinner with a choice and gleeful party. On these
days his own food almost turned his stomach ; he
eat it with an ill will, troubled with dainty fancies,
and in the evening he could not settle to his
work.

His spirit was embittered ; the pay he got for
his work bore no proportion to the sum he would
have needed to gratify his desires ; and what then
was the use of working at all ! Then he would go

out and mix in the crowd or stand at the doors of
the theatres where the people waited in a line to
make their way in. All these folks — hundreds
and thousands of his fellow-citizens—had, besides
the actual necessaries of life, some superfluous
coin to spare for amusement. He alone had not;
and he wandered about thinly clad, in the cold
and mist, dreaming fondly of the stifling heat and
atmosphere of a play-house. He stood watching
the masks who sprang out of the hired carriages
and vanished into the great theatre — *la Scala* —
figures of women, wrapped in white wadded cloaks
that made them look like huge bundles; pink or
sky-blue, or cherry-colored silk ancles and satin
boots supported the unwieldy looking masses with
pattering steps ; impatient when the crowd delayed
them in their rush, eager to fling themselves into
that vortex of gaiety, dancing and folly. Or he saw
the grand ladies who got out of old family coaches in
full evening dress, with long skirts of velvet or satin,
and who were only going to look on with dignified
propriety from their boxes ; and these, as they
swept by him, would leave a strong fragrance in
the air. The men who accompanied them were
shrouded in overcoats down to their heels and but-

toned to the chin, but their lavender gloves and
gibbus hats betrayed the hidden splendors of a
dress-coat, with white tie, and snowy shirt-front.
Giovanni pictured them to himself when they got
inside, shedding their chrysalis-cases like huge
black butterflies ; in his fancy they were radiant
and handsome, and bitter melancholy gnawed at
his heart.   He shivered in his thin cloak that did
not keep out the frost, and hurried off with his
teeth chattering, to a squalid coffee-shop where he
would drink a glass of hot punch to warm himself,
thaw for a few minutes in the thick atmosphere
reeking with spirits, and tobacco smoke — altogether unwholesome and suffocating — and then
go home to bed that he might not see others revelling in the pleasures that were denied to him.

But even in his wretched loft he could hear the
shouts of the maskers, the rumble of the carriages,
dulled by the snow or made louder by the sharp
ring of the frozen ground.   The festivities pursued him even in his bed ; and as he lay curled up
to keep himself warm, with his head under the
scanty coverlet to shelter himself from the piercing draughts that whistled in at every crack, he
pictured in his mind all those unknown joys of

life, a thousand times more delightful than the reality. He saw palaces like those of the Arabian Nights, gorgeous with impossible splendors; women of ideal beauty; a radiant display of white shoulders, rich stuffs, magnificent jewels, and all the. intoxications of love. And when he was weary of the secret struggle and ungratified imaginings, the final days of madness came, when from morning till night, the carriages full of maskers drove about the streets to the sound of bands of music, when the shops were shut, and their signs were hung with white cloth to protect them against the pelting of sugar-plums. Then there was no work done. In the roadway and on the balconies every one was idle, and every one was shouting. Comfits filled the air, poured out in sacksful, in hundreds of pounds weight, as merrily and carelessly as though they cost nothing; flowers were flung about, oranges, bonbons — for the mere sake of throwing away something, the sheer delight of spending broadcast. It was as if the whole population, over-burdened with unexpected and superfluous wealth, were in a hurry to be rid of it and were revelling in the waste of this plethora of riches. The bands played triumphant marches,

every voice was raised in one mighty and deafen-
ing shout.   Lords and laborers, men and women,
all went crazy together; danced in the market-
places, lighted bonfires, wore masks, and demeaned
themselves like wild creatures.   Giovanni felt that
he alone could have no part in this festival of joy
and plenty; he alone was cold and hungry; and
it filled him with such wrath and bitterness that
in the midst of this universal madness of mirth,
he was well nigh mad with melancholy.

Another season of misery was midsummer —
the intolerable midsummer of Milan.   Born and
bred in the country, loving its pure air, its green
hills, its cool shelter under the shade of spreading
trees, the very first spring-tide made him home-
sick; and as the summer went on this craving for
fresh air became almost an illness.   Every one
went away to the baths, to the hills, to the sea, to
the lakes; and Giovanni met no one in the streets
of Milan but a few hard-worked and weary beings
like himself— men of business, merchants whose
families were away, and who joined them every
Saturday, or employés who were only waiting to
get their month's leave to make some long excur-
sion.   He alone had no one to go to on a holi-

day, and expected no leave, but must go on working, working, every day to earn the next day's
bread.   His room was unbearable, the heat was
intense to a degree that made it painful to breathe;
the sweat poured down his face as he sat writing
and fell in drops on the paper; his body felt on
fire; he was always thirsty and swallowed glass
after glass of lukewarm water that he loathed, that
made him feel sick, and that threw him into violent perspirations and weakened and depressed
him.

In the evening he took long walks in search
of fresh air; but on the high-roads, scorched by
the day's sun, his feet sank up to the ancles in
dust, and raised such a cloud that it choked him
and powdered him from head to foot; if he went
to walk in the suburbs he ran through the whole
gamut of horrible smells.   After facing the sicken-
ing odors of a tanner's yard he met the sour fumes
of a dyer's that made him choke; further on the
fetid smell of steeping flax came up from a spinning shed, and even the market-gardens reeked
with manures and loams.   Everything that could
spoil and decompose under the tropical heat ex-
haled its own peculiar stench; the butchers' shops,

the slaughter-houses, the dairies, the cheese stores, the gutters, the canal, the heaps of sweepings outside the houses — each and all stank and contributed to poison the air with a taint of rottenness and filth that made his gorge rise.

The few men of the better class who remained in the town went about with their ties undone, fanning themselves with their hats; the workmen wore only their trousers and shirts with the sleeves turned up, and the open collars showing their hairy chests; the door-keepers came out to sit in the streets in the dusk, in the least permissible amount of clothing and with bare feet in their wooden shoes. On Sundays every one escaped, going out by dozens to the taverns and gardens within easy reach, to sit under the dreary little arbors in a back plot that make believe to be country. There they got bad food and worse drink, and panted with the heat and dust; and then crowded into omnibuses to return to the town, puffing and perspiring, suffocating in an atmosphere of steam, smoke, and tipsiness. On one occasion only Giovanni had made such an expedition and it had given him an attack of fever.

Exhausted and jarred in every nerve he was more wretched than ever in the atmosphere to which his country lungs could not by any means adapt themselves; he had fevered visions of wide fields, of clear waters, of trees and shade, and of burning noons on the silent heights and in the pure air of the hills. He dreamed of a little white house with green shutters in a wide and lonely plain; dreamed of it, gloated over it, with the passion of a lover; and whenever he saw a coach loaded with luggage on its way to the station — to the country, where the world was green and the air was clear, he felt a wild desire to hang on to it like a street boy. It left him sadder, more out of heart; and he cursed the fate that held him shut up and pining miserably in a town where he had hoped to find fortune and fame and all that could make life sweet.

The first time that his master put the conduct of a case into his hands Giovanni thought that he had attained the goal of his ambition. It was a civil action between two small proprietors as to a party-wall; a squabble about a childish difference and entirely devoid of interest. But the young advocate threw himself into it heart and soul; he

investigated the history of the two parties and of
their respective properties, going back beyond the
memory of man.   He brought an infinity of zeal
to bear upon it, made voluminous notes, studied
the question with a thoroughness and perspicacity
that were, literally enough, "worthy of a better
cause."   In the evenings, instead of plodding on
at his usual work of translating or copying, he
went over the whole business again and again. He
prepared the speech he intended to make, improv-
ing it, and adding particulars.   Then he wanted to
try how it would sound, and to rehearse his ges-
tures, so rising to his feet, serious but not solemn,
he bowed to an imaginary crowd and began with
great simplicity and dignity to harangue the lasts
and sabots that hung round the room. By degrees
he grew more animated; he could fancy that
among all those wooden feet he saw Rachel's
bright face, smiling at him to encourage him; his
words came fluently and in elegant periods, as he
pictured her among the audience; he added fire, he
raised his voice, till at length the startled last-
maker put out his night-capped head to ask if the
house were on fire.

When at length he went to bed, tired and ex-

cited, he felt the spirit of a great advocate burning within him, and indulged in intoxicating
dreams of a success that should make his reputation, thinking of the impression that this dazzling
triumph would be sure to produce at Fontanetto.
He could see his patrons all bowing down to him,
Pedrotti holding out his hands in apologetic supplication, and all the gossips of the hamlet coming
out of their shops and exclaiming :

"It is the Dottorino's son—Mazza, the great
lawyer ! What an honor for the place ! and now
he is going to marry the daughter of Signor Pedrotti of the castle !" And his mind wandered off
into thoughts of his love — he and Rachel were
starting in a coach for their wedding journey—he
jumped in after her — and shut the door. . . .

And in fact, when the case came on Giovanni
spoke with all the skill of an experienced pleader.
A senior who happened to be present shook him
warmly by the hand and his client paid him hand-
somely. But, unluckily, outside the court no one
cared a straw for the case of the party-wall; the
newspapers of course did not mention it, and
within three days this great event in our hero's
life was totally forgotten and had left no trace, no

alteration whatever in the young clerk's life or prospects, beyond a small handful of coins in his purse. At first he found it hard to believe this. When he entered the shop and bid the worthy man good evening he felt that he was condescending and thought to himself: "If only he could know what I am!" and in the morning, as he sat eating his broth in a corner near the fire, he could not help remembering an old peasant woman who had an earthenware plate which she used to show to everybody, saying:

"Do you see that? Out of that plate Carlo Alberto eat two eggs. He eat for all the world like you or me. And afterwards I was told it was the King. Madonna Santa!"

CHAPTER XVIII.

BUT the days and months went by. More than a year had gone and the last-maker had not yet begun to wonder that Giovanni eat just like other people. Indeed, the good woman was apt to hint without any reticence that he eat a good deal more than some people. At the same time he had enlarged the circle of his acquaintance; other cases of an unimportant kind had been intrusted to him, and he had become friendly with some of his clients. His fellow-clerks had listened to his speeches, had enthusiastically admired his talents and had offered to introduce him to signor so and so, or the cavaliere such an one—persons of influence. Giovanni had been only too glad to accept. But what endless trouble and vexation those visits cost him! He had to procure gloves and ties; he could not do without a shiny hat and a well-starched shirt front; then he had to get new shoes when, but for this, the pair he had would have lasted another month. Indeed, for one call he

had to pay on a certain commendatore, he was
under the necessity of borrowing a pocket-hand-
kerchief of his landlady, because his own were all
too shabby.   It was quite new and rather thick,
and it made his coat bulge out as if he had a roll
in his pocket; and when he had occasion to use
it it came out in creases and corners like paper,
and crackled as much.   And after all this worry,
the outcome of these introductions rarely led to
any result.   The individual to whom some zeal-
ous friend presented him with an enthusiastic
enumeration of his merits, his distinction at college,
his talents, his industry, his general ill-luck, etc.,
etc., would bow and reply:

"Bravo! Bravo! I am delighted. . ."

"If at any time you can use your influence. . ."
the friend would hint; and to this direct appeal
the man in power — real or fancied — would
vaguely respond: "Oh! certainly, by all means.
I will bear it in mind. . ." and Giovanni never
heard of him again, unless the friend who had introduced him happened to remind him that he really
ought to call again at a house where he had been
so well received.   In specially favorable cases he
was consulted as to some old-standing law-suit, or

was employed in some petty case or some dis-
creditable affair. But he always threw himself into
it with zeal; he was commonly paid rather less
than a stranger, in consideration of his intimacy,
or the introduction, or what not — and there the
matter ended. At last he began to feel disappointment weighing on him heavily.   He put so much
thought and so much energy into the little he had
to do, that it was inevitable that he should himself
think highly of his work.   He knew that he had
done his very best, and he said to himself: " If,
with so much hard work, I have failed to make
myself known, there is an end of it. I never shall
succeed."

And then he would contemplate the possibilities of a long life of sacrifice and toil, availing
simply to maintain himself in dreary sufficiency;
he thought of Rachel who, never hearing his name
mentioned, would at last marry some one else;
and he pictured her in all the magnificence of a
rich woman, while he must continue to grind his
heart out merely to have bread to eat while life
lasted.

One day of extreme depression it occurred to
him :   " Women are said to be all-powerful.   I

wonder if I could find one to take me up." And
he got himself introduced to the lady of a great
promoter of railway speculations. She was a
woman of an original and independent character,
who had not thought the blessing of the church
at all necessary on her union with the wealthy
banker. Giovanni was young and handsome and
found favor in her eyes. She promised him the
banker for a client, assuring him that he was a
most litigious man who did not care what he spent
but must secure a clever lawyer, and would certainly give the preference to one of her recom-
mendation. But Giovanni must come often to the
house, so that the great man might see him and
take a fancy to him, and then. . . promises without end; none of which did the lady think of
keeping but those made by her black eyes and
which depended solely on herself. But by the
end of a week Giovanni was so thoroughly disgusted that he vowed never to set foot in the
house again.

This brief interlude had not had the slightest
effect on his feelings towards Rachel. Indeed,
when it struck him to think of her as weeping and
despairing, in the compunction of his remorseful

soul he felt that he loved her more than ever for
the grief he had caused her; and when he was
alone he went down on his knees to the maiden
image he had conjured up, and besought her pardon and lost himself in protestations, and vows
and bitter tears.

CHAPTER XIX.

AFTER this experience he went through a long
period of deep dejection; he was not even excited
when he had a case put into his hands. All his
illusions were sere and leafless, as it were, and he
knew full well that these petty causes would never
enable him to add one cell to the hive. However,
he got a good many, and by degrees he lost the
habit of wearing patched shoes, and threadbare
coats, and he quitted his loft at the last-maker's.
But with the misery of his young days the illusions too had vanished, the dreams of future great-
ness; and he had fallen into the prosaic truism of
dreary mediocrity.

"I have mistaken my vocation," he would think to himself. "The law is not my road to riches." And he felt utterly mortified by the reflection that three years had gone by and he was not yet in a position to present himself at the castle of Fontanneto without raising a smile of contempt for his miserable earnings of three hundred francs a month. Then he became possessed by the strange idea of going back to his old penurious way of living, so as to put by a certain sum and speculate in stocks. He knew of some colossal fortunes having been made in this way, and he said to himself: "Who knows?" During those first years of extreme poverty he had found out the art of living on the least possible pittance, and now, fired by his desire to win Rachel before she was snatched away from him, he found no difficulty in renouncing his new and comparatively luxurious way of living; he did it with enthusiasm, rejoicing in his self-inflicted privations, and he gloated like a miser over each crown that he added to his savings. At the end of a year he had accumulated about one thousand five hundred francs, when one day he received a letter from his father, who wrote as follows:

" I am overwhelmed with debts and infirmities, and now that I am no longer able to amuse these gentlemen by my jokes and stories they have ceased to give me dinners. I have no great faith in the generosity of human nature, and still less in the ties of blood; still I hope that to save your father from beggary which would be a discredit to you, you will contrive to provide for his declining years. I never set up for being a loving parent, but at any rate for twelve years of your life I kept you in more or less decency, and it is hardly likely that you will have me on your hands for so long. . ."

Giovanni could not help a shudder as he read this letter; he felt as if an abyss had opened at his feet. He had made for himself a slender foothold and this brought the certainty that it would henceforth forever fail him. Whatever he might earn for the future it could never be more than enough for himself and his father, and if he now parted with the sum he had laid by, he could never hope to replace it. At the same time it did not for an instant occur to him to evade the duty. It was long since Giovanni had wept, but he shed bitter tears over this letter. His father had eaten

and drunken and made merry, while he had been
toiling at this petty earning and saving, to enable
him to win the girl he loved; and now his father
could claim the fruits of his labor and self-denial,
and say to him: "Give up your hopes of your
own free will, or I will snatch them from you by
the exhibition of my indigence."

His whole soul rebelled at this injustice and
quaked at the burden thus laid upon him; and
when he presently enclosed his savings in a registered letter he felt none of the satisfaction of having done a good action; nor, indeed, any pity for
the doctor, but only a void in his heart and an
utter despair of the future, with an incurable bitterness of regret for the hopes he was burying.
As he angrily set his seal in the melted wax, he
muttered: "There is a curse on it!"

It was a curse, a fatality, which pursued him
as it had pursued so many others, and which con-
demned him to live unknown, wasting his talents,
his learning — and all his superior qualities.

From that time, completely disheartened by this
fatal blow, he abandoned himself to his fate and
hoped no longer. He would remember his dreams
of good fortune and think of Rachel as of a fair

but shattered vision. He closed his mind with positive terror to the thought that he might one day meet her as the wife of another. All he asked was never to see her again. He felt that he could not face her without a sense of failure and disgrace. He had not kept his boastful promises; he had been too presumptuous and his failure proved him to have been ignorant as well. At the bottom of his heart, to be sure, he did not believe this; but, after all, no man is allowed to go out on the house tops and cry out: "Wait, only wait till I am a great man. Let me do this or that, and you will see!" We cannot do without the aid of circumstances; all we ourselves can do is to take advantage of them. But circumstances had done nothing to help Giovanni.

CHAPTER XX.

ONE day Signor Berti sent for Giovanni and communicated to him the particulars of a case of murder. A tavern-keeper had stabbed a gentleman's servant; it was a vulgar row, there was no opening for a brilliant defence, and the great lawyer was content to hand it over to his young deputy. Giovanni set to work to study the case with the dillettante interest that he always brought to his work; but it was impossible to deny the guilt of the accused. Not only was it perfectly clear from the evidence, but the murderer himself confessed it. Besides this he was a most impracticable client; when Giovanni first saw him he was painfully impressed by this. The man sat in the darkest corner of his cell, with his elbows on his knees and his jaws resting on his clenched fists which pushed up his cheeks till his eyes were almost closed. He was about sixty years of age, but he looked much older, for he was bald and his beard was white. He had a cold, hard stare, and the deeply wrinkled features of a violent nature. The young lawyer's presence seemed to confirm him in his tenacity; he showed not the smallest interest in his visit, and when Giovanni explained that it was his duty to defend him, he shrugged his shoulders and replied :

" I killed the man, I do not deny it ; I need no defence."

However Giovanni might cross-question him he could get nothing more out of him. This extraordinary indifference seemed very unnatural to the young pleader. He turned to the gaoler.

"What does the prisoner say about his trial ?"

" He says nothing, for he never speaks a word."

" What does he do all day ?"

" He sits in that corner, just as you see him. Sometimes he reads or scribbles on the wall with a pencil."

Giovanni asked to see the book he read. It was a ragged and dirty Bible which opened of its own accord at the place where the parable is told of the rich man who, having a hundred sheep, robbed a poor man of his one ewe lamb. On the wall too were mottoes in abuse of the rich, some quoted from the scriptures or from popular songs; while others were evidently of his own invention. On a door post he had scribbled: "In the heart of the rich a serpent dwells." Above his bed: "The devil puts his demons into the white skin of the rich to torment the poor." And below this he had written: "If you are noble and have money to spend make the most of your thieves' luck in this world, for in the next you will serve for coals to warm the poor withal." On one side was a list of the names which the French revolution had made famous even in Italy: *Marat, Robespierre, Danton.* Above all, in large letters, he had scrawled: "*Evviva!*" (Hurrah!) and at the bottom: "Everlasting glory!"

Giovanni turned to the prisoner and said:

"You are a socialist then?"

The man did not seem to understand and made no reply.

"You do not approve of the world as it is?" the young lawyer went on, "and you would like to alter it?"

The old man vehemently clutched at the pitcher that stood beside him and flung it over, heedless of the water that poured over the tiled floor.

"Ah! you would like to upset it?" Giovanni asked.

"Ah!" sighed the old man; then crouching till his shoulders were up to his ears, he groaned more deeply. "But what then, — what good would it do?"

"Then some rich man has done you an injury?" asked Giovanni. The prisoner drew himself up indignantly, almost threateningly exclaiming:

"No one has done me any wrong; do you hear? I am poor, but I am respected. I have killed a man. Well what then? But there is nothing against my character."

Giovanni could make nothing of him, for the man he had stabbed was a poor servant who had gone into the tavern to drink, and the old man, the instant he saw him, without picking any quarrel, had rushed upon him shrieking :

"Thief! villain! slave to the rich, I will give it you — I will teach you!" And he had stabbed him in the throat with a knife that he had seized off the counter. There were five witnesses to the fact who happened to be in the shop, and the man himself made no denial or excuse.

Giovanni, at his wits' end, demanded a medical examination. He could discover no plea for his client; but his fixed idea evidently was a detestation of the upper classes; this might be a mania or an old grudge. In the first case a medical examination would procure him justice; in the second he might be able to find out his secret and perhaps to save him yet; and meanwhile he had gained time.

Giovanni did not let the grass grow under his feet. This violent and unexpected assassination must have been planned, and if it were premeditated it must have had a motive. Now the only motive that the accused would confess to was his hatred of the rich; he had killed the man because he was the servant of a rich master. But a few enquiries sufficed to prove that many of his customers were gentlemen's servants, and that though the man had been apt to treat them roughly he had never insulted or provoked them. Thus it was this particular servant that he had hated; and in the reason for that hatred there might be an excuse, or at any rate an extenuation of the crime. The accused, however, persisted in declaring that he had not been acquainted with his victim; that he had never seen him till that day. To detect the real motive that had prompted him to the crime it was necessary to investigate his past history; but the criminal had moved about so constantly within the last few years that his present landlord knew him but slightly, and knew nothing of his previous life. Giovanni worked back on the traces to his former lodgings; from *Porta Romana* he went to *San Celso*. There his client had lived for six months; but his business had at that time been in another street until he moved about six months since when he had taken the house, a tavern at the *Porta Romana*. Finally, by dint of running from door to door, in a blind alley near the *Porta Ticinese*, where the man had lived many years before, Giovanni discovered that at that time he had had a daughter. They had quitted the premises suddenly, without waiting for the end of the quarter, but they had left no debts, and the rent had been paid up. Now what had become of the daughter? Giovanni went to the prison and asked the criminal.

"My daughter is dead," said the old man, "and you will allow me to request that you will not go prying into my private affairs." The old man had turned very red, and seemed so excited that Giovanni was convinced he had laid his finger on an old sore. The murdered man was no doubt the seducer of the girl. The medical enquiry resulted in a report that the accused was in the full possession of his faculties. In a few days the trial would be reopened.

CHAPTER XXI.

MEANWHILE the newspapers, in stating that the prisoner had been remanded pending a medical enquiry claimed on his behalf by his counsel, had of course reported the reasons for this demand; which were Galbusera's invectives against the upper classes, and the ravings that he had scrawled over the walls of his prison. And this was quite enough to rouse public curiosity on the subject which till then had not excited any interest. This curiosity was greatly increased when it suddenly was rumored that the further course of the trial would gravely implicate the representative of a noble Milanese family, who was notorious not merely for the historic name he bore but for his ostentatious wealth, his love-affairs, and his extravagant whims, which had not unfrequently afforded matter for public comment. As always happens, the newspapers vied with each other as to who should have the earliest and fullest particulars of the scandal now in the wind; and the name of Giovanni Mazza, the young lawyer, was in every mouth, coupled with that of the gentleman who had been summoned to give evidence for the defense. It became known that the discovery of the secret motive for the crime was due to the indefatigable energy and acumen of the avvocato Mazza and popular imagination once excited, invented a perfect romance about the young man who had, unaided, worked up and completed the case for his client, and by his personal courage and zeal had defeated the influence which certain persons in high places had attempted to exert in order to suppress the facts. The story which the newspapers now printed and which the trial confirmed was briefly as follows. About twelve years before the commission of the crime Galbusera was keeping the wine shop near the Porta Ticinese; he was at that time a widower with a daughter of fifteen

who was apprenticed to a dressmaker. A coachman named Teodoro Donadio was in the habit of
frequenting the tavern very regularly every evening and before long it was evident that he was
paying his addresses to the young girl. Galbusera
interfered, saying that the women of his family
had always been well-conducted, that this child
was the pride of his life. If he wanted to marry
her he had better say so, and give them the opportunity of knowing something about him;
otherwise he would not allow the girl to compro-
mise herself by listening to his gallantries. Donadio had asked a short time to make up his mind
and a few days later he had come back accompanied by a tobacconist who lived in the same
street, who was charged with the commission of
asking the hand of Maddalena Galbusera for his
friend. Donadio added that he was in service in
a highly respectable house, that his wages were
sufficient to maintain a family and that his master
would make no difficulties in the way of his marrying. Galbusera, however, desired the tobacconist to request an interview with the Marchese
Trestelle, Donadio's master, to make enquiries as
to the coachman's character and to find out

whether there really was no danger of his losing his place in consequence of his marriage. The tobacconist had not been able to see the marquis; but he had seen his secretary who had made a note of his enquiries and on the following day he had himself fetched the answer; the master spoke highly of Donadio and made no objection to the marriage. The wedding was fixed to take place at Michaelmas because at that time the marquis would be able to lodge the couple in the attic of one of his houses. There would be five months to wait but that would not be too long to prepare the modest outfit, and Maddalena was so young that her father was glad to postpone it till she should have passed her sixteenth birthday.

When everything was thus settled Donadio had taken to going every evening to fetch his sweetheart home from her work, and not unfrequently he would meet her in the morning and walk with her to the seamstress'. He spent less and less time in his father-in-law's shop, and ended by never sitting there at all, since he saw Maddalena out of doors and preferred having her to himself to meeting her in the presence of the

neighbors.   When she went in the girl would say:
" He came to fetch me, and brought me to the
door."

At last, however, when they had been betrothed about four months, for a whole fortnight
Donadio failed to appear at all ; Maddalena was
melancholy and her father saw that she was constantly in tears.   There must have been some
quarrel.   He questioned the girl who at first
denied that she was in any trouble, but on being
pressed had confessed everything.

Not long after Donadio had begun to fetch her
from the dressmaker's, as they were on their way
home, they had met the marquis in one of the least
frequented streets of the city.   There was in fact no
one to be seen, and the gentleman had condescended to ask the coachman if this was his sweetheart and to pay her some compliments.   Then he
had met them again, more than once, and the
servant would stand aside and leave his master to
chat with the young girl ; the marquis was much
handsomer and gentler and better mannered than
the coachman, and the little needlewoman had listened only too readily to his fine speeches.   Mar-
quises and counts had married humble girls before

now, and at fifteen nothing seems impossible. Besides, the nobleman promised . . . only on account
of his high rank he could not make it known till
the last moment . . . they must let the world believe that the coachman was her lover . . . And
the marquis would drive out early in the day and
wait outside the city gates; thither Donadio
would conduct her and then she spent the day with
his master.

But about a month before Michaelmas master
and man had vanished. The girl had gone back
to her work and her mistress had treated her but
coolly after her long spell of idleness, while her
companions gossiped and taunted her about her
grand acquaintance which they had not failed to
find out. Seeing days and months slip by without any sign of the marquis the poor child had
broken down, and had confided her woes to her
mistress who had told her that a fortnight since
the Marchese Trestelle had married the daughter
of a rich Genoese banker, and after a short wedding tour, had settled at Genoa near his bride's
family. As to Donadio, whether he was with his
master or no, he had left Milan.

On hearing his daughter's confession Galbusera

had at once left the neighborhood, without waiting till the end of the term, to hide his own and
his child's disgrace. The dressmaker to whom
Maddalena had also confessed her misery, recommended an old nurse living at Monza, where the
poor child would be taken care of and remain unknown. Two months later she had died there, after
the premature birth of her infant.

For ten years Galbusera had chewed the cud
of his wrath, grief and shame ; avoiding every face
he knew, changing his residence whenever he sus-
pected that he had been recognized, and thrilling
at the thought of some day meeting the marquis or
Donadio.   Then, one day, Donadio had gone into
the shop and he had stabbed him.

It would be impossible to describe the excitement produced in Milan by the revelation of these
facts; indeed not only in Milan ; all Italy talked
of this trial.   It took place at a time when politics
happened to be devoid of interest and the papers
flung themselves greedily on this exciting drama
of crime.   Party spirit, of course, and as usual,
inflamed their partisanship. The republican and
social papers spoke of the assassin as a hero, and
lauded him to the skies — nay even the mottoes

he had scribbled on the wall and the grammarless notes that he spent his time in writing from his cell. The conservative organs, on the contrary, did more than insinuate that the intrigue attributed to the Marchese Trestelle was a device adopted to extract money from him, and to throw discredit on the class to which he belonged.

To Giovanni the certainty of having the eyes of the country fixed upon him was a powerful incentive and at the end of the first day of the trial he was himself astonished at the fervor of his eloquence and the cogency of his arguments. The examination of the Marchese Trestelle — of which the result was telegraphed the same evening to all the important newspapers throughout Italy—was a triumph for the young lawyer; with admirable skill he contrived to extract from the witness a full admission of the truth, and so happy was he in his address, sarcastic and indignant by turns, that he subdued the haughtiness of his witness most effectually, and heaped on him all the scornful condemnation that he had so righteously deserved. The summing up with which he closed his defence surpassed the expectations of the audience, and was long quoted and remembered as a triumph of forensic skill. It was not so much a defence, argued out on legal grounds, as an elaborate psychological study, in which the criminal and his victim, the seducer and the young girl, were drawn as typical personages, and the whole subject was treated from a lofty stand-point. The case, which at first had been no more than a mere vulgar scandal was transfigured in his hands and assumed a totally new aspect; it was a tragedy fraught with solemn lessons.

When Giovanni sat down exhausted with excitement, the presiding judge found it impossible to check the applause of the audience. Everyone present — lawyers, magistrates, critics, were agreed that a great genius here stood revealed. Fortune favored him; the verdict was not, it is true, an acquittal; but the premeditation was ignored, the provocation estimated as almost irresistible and the penalty made as light as the law would allow.

CHAPTER XXII.

THE press gave the new legal star a dinner and his contemporaries in the profession did the same; and as he sat at these banquets he remembered with a smile that dinner at five francs a head which he had given to his fellow-clerks, and all the humiliation and sacrifices it had cost him. Once more the hopes that he had buried rose from the grave and stood before him, more enchanting than ever because this fame had come to him suddenly, in a day as it were, when it had seemed to have deserted him forever. Henceforth his position was assured; the future smiled upon him and money would not fail to flow in. Whenever he read an article in a paper sounding his praises he thought to himself: "Rachel will see this, her father will even read it," and his fancy looked back on the dreary autumn day when he had said as he drove past the castle: "And she too; well she shall see." And now — now she would see what he had been able to do. "It has cost me dear, but I have succeeded," he said to himself; and he was proud of his fortitude and of the privations he had endured. He was happy to feel how young he was and how much of his life lay before him.

Dating from the success of the Galbusera trial a new life of incessant business and bustle began for the young lawyer, in which the twenty-four hours of the day were not long enough for all he had to do in them. Clients flocked to him and he was appointed referee in election matters by his political party. He was invited to contribute to various legal periodicals, and wrote some articles on a scheme for certain reforms which were discussed in all the leading papers. His talents and his theories, which till now had been ignored, were fully revealed and in a short time his name was universally famous.

During the five years that he had spent in Berti's office his principal had never proposed to introduce him to his wife. He had seen her come into her husband's rooms several times, with a great rustle of silk skirts, leaving in her wake a strong perfume of violets which had given the young clerk a high idea of her elegance. She had

glanced at him now and again through the meshes
of her lace veil, but had never spoken to him.
But the day after the famous trial of Galbusera
his master said to him:

"My wife desires to make your acquaintance.
Come to-morrow evening to take tea with us, and
I will introduce you to her."

He and Berti had never been intimate; the
senior had always spoken to him with the familiar-
ity of a leader to his subaltern, his inferior, and
not that of a friend. And Giovanni had seen
enough of the world to understand the meaning
of this change; he smiled at the idea that so
clever a man, who had known him well for five
years, should have waited to appreciate him at his
true worth until public opinion had set its seal
upon his merits. His introduction into the house
of so distinguished a man and his presentation to
the lady who, as he judged, must be double his
own age, gave him something to think about.
Signora Berti was in fact past forty; but she had
no children and was a handsome woman; she took
the greatest care of her beauty too, dressed elegantly and went to the theatre and to balls in low
dresses, with short sleeves and with flowers in her

hair; she danced, flirted with men younger than
herself, liked their attentions and let them know
that she did.   Giovanni did not fail to understand
from her airs and glances and style of dress that
the lady still maintained her pretensions to youth-
fulness and he found some difficulty in reconciling
these pretensions with her undoubted age, and
with her dignity as the wife of his principal—two
things which kept him at bay.   When he arrived
at Berti's house the lawyer received him as a com-
rade; he went forward to meet him with both
hands out, took him confidentially by the arm,
and as he led him through the length of two
rooms to introduce him to his wife, he said:
"Here we are friends.   We are not principal
and deputy; those I receive in my own house
are my equals..." And stopping to press his
hand once more he added: "and my colleagues."

Then he went on to say that the Galbusera
case had placed Mazza among the most distinguished advocates of Milan and discussed and
criticised his method of defense, comparing it with
his own, analyzing his arguments and admiring
his ingenuity.   Giovanni was deeply touched, and

warmly returned the friendly grasp of the man
whom he had hitherto thought of only as a superficial rhetorician but whom he now began to see
in a new light. The stirring appeals for which
Berti had for so many years been famous were not
mere studied effects; he was really a man of feeling.
In spite of his fifty years he had a poetic fancy,
passionate emotions, and a romantic nature.   It
was a real effort to him to keep up his dignity before the youths in his office, for he loved young
people and liked to join in their amusements; he
had all the eagerness and venturesome spirit of
youth.   When he first heard Giovanni's style of
defense, devoid of those declamatory effects by
which he could draw tears from his audience and
melt even the jury, he had found it cold: " He
has no blood in his veins," he had thought. ·" He
does not know how to move his hearers; he will
never do anything to save a client."   But when
he had heard the young advocate plead the cause
of Galbusera and achieve such success by the
mere statement of facts, he was deeply impressed
and had felt a genuine pleasure in his subaltern's
triumph.   Though he himself was a born rhetorician and could do no less than remain so, he

could appreciate the merit of a more realistic method of argument.

The lady's cordiality was less genuine. Still, she was really pleased at having in her drawing-room the young lawyer who was just then the most talked-of man in Milan; but her satisfaction arose from vanity and not from sympathy with him. She, like her husband, had youthful instincts; but in him they were the outcome of an enthusiastic and generous nature whose illusions age can never altogether dispel; in her they were only vanity and coquetry. During the whole evening she devoted her attention almost exclusively to the illustrious visitor; she introduced him to everyone and when the ladies invited him to their evenings " at home " she answered for him : " Yes — I will bring him with me on Tuesday, or on Sunday. I intend to introduce him everywhere as my husband's pupil."

Then she would add with a laugh, as if she were saying something supremely absurd: " I shall play mother to him." And Giovanni would be constrained to say that she was too young and handsome and that such a mother inspired feelings

that were anything rather than reverent . . . very
different. . .

However, sometimes under her protection and
sometimes alone, Giovanni made the round of
Milan society. His handsome face and unaffected
good manners, his dignified reserve, pleasant ease
and above all his genuine wit made him a favorite
with all. Men consulted him on grave political or
social matters and thought highly of his judgment.
The young married ladies lamented his inability
to dance, declaring that at his age it was unpar-
donable, and inviting him to try a polka or a
quadrille under pretence of teaching him, but in
reality because they liked to walk round a room
arm in arm with him, to talk to him, to hear his
compliments which were always fresher than the
stereotype formulas to which they were accustomed
However, Giovanni did learn to dance a little, and
during the next carnival indulged in that exercise
though in moderation, and became one of the most
fashionable young men of the Milan beau monde.

But the establishment of an office of his own
with suitable lodgings, his more elegant style of
dress, his dinners in a better supplied and more
fashionably frequented eating-house, all proved

costly. He still had his old horror of being a
parasite like his father and of its ever being said to
him: "You live on others, as the Dottorino did
before you." Good Heavens! To escape this
he lavished flowers, artistic trifles and boxes at the
theatres on the families who invited him to their
dinners and soirées, and all this ran away with his
money. His earnings barely sufficed to meet his
expenses and to supply his father's demands; and
in the midst of his triumphs he was still far—very
far — from Signor Pedrotti's ideal of a rich husband for his daughter. But this thought was no
longer so much in the foreground of his mind;
the memory of Rachel, though it was still one of
his fondest thoughts—when he thought of her,
haunted him with less insistency than of old. To
marry her was still his ruling purpose, a compact,
as it were, with himself, a decree of destiny; but
he no longer felt any impatient ardor to attain that
end — nay, other ardors and different yearnings
had taken possession of his soul.

CHAPTER XXIII.

SINCE Giovanni had been released from the
wearisome necessity of providing every day for
the next day's needs, since he had gained the
leisure of an easier existence and saw himself surrounded by luxury and beauty, his vigorous·and
unspoiled youth had waked up to the thirst for
pleasure which was strong in proportion to the
length of its enforced torpor. He felt all the fascinations of the hundred women who smiled upon
him and gave him their hand; he gazed with a
sort of intoxication at their white shoulders and
saw them again in his dreams. The brief flirtations
with the sempstress or the milliner who had smiled
from time to time on the poor clerk, without occupying either his heart or his fancy, had no
longer any charms for him. His nature was poetical
and a love of all that was fair and refined was in-
stinctive with him. He liked well-born and well-
bred women, witty and well dressed; he liked to
breathe the same air, to lounge at their feet on

thick carpets, to sit by their side on velvet sofas, to inhale the fragrance of their hair and their gloves. He panted for his share of happiness, for some stormy romance; he felt that he was living in an atmosphere from which it might be evolved, and his vehement imagination loved to picture it as full of emotion and ecstasy.

One evening at a ball, when he had hidden himself, as he thought, behind two camellia shrubs, to indulge for a time in these visions of possible bliss, he saw a beautiful arm invitingly extended and a sweetly regretful voice said plaintively:

"For pity's sake come and dance this quadrille; I was obliged to go way to fasten up my hair and I have lost my partner."

He started up in astonishment, gazing at that arm, those shoulders, that throat, all that expanse of warm white — the rose-tipped creaminess of a blonde beauty — which came upon him like the realization of his dreams. He obeyed the appeal in stricken silence and got through the figures of the dance he knew not how; never taking his eyes off his partner. He felt suffocating.

He had met this lady on various occasions, indeed he knew her and had been at her house,

and he had seen that she was handsome; but he
had never before felt the smallest emotion from her
beauty. They had been capital friends on the
terms of good fellowship which a woman of the
world knows so well how to establish with a man
she gets on with and in speaking of her Giovanni
had often said: " I like her because she never
wants me to court her. I can talk to her as I
should to a man."

But now—in this moment of intoxication he felt
as if her beauty had been created for him; that
this fair revelation was a sort of outcome of his
imaginings; that he had evoked it and it had appeared at his bidding. He could not say anything and looked anxious and disturbed.

" What ails you Avvocato ?" asked the countess.

" Oh ! you are too beautiful !" sighed Giovanni
in the low helpless tones of a man carried away by
his passion.

The lady stood stupefied; it was as though she
had had a sudden blow. She felt in an instant that
she ought to have resented this address and re-
proved her audacious companion, or turn her fair
shoulders on him and leave him to repent of his

boldness; but then she felt no resentment. In fact she had had a blow — an electric shock; the sultry oppression that troubled Giovanni fell upon her too. They finished the quadrille in silence and agitation — that emotional silence which is more eloquent and more explicit than any words; their hands trembled as they clasped, lingered, and parted slowly, and their eyes met and could not fall, like magnetized needles; their hearts throbbed under the weight of an obscure melancholy, an inexplicable dread; and she could have wept passionate tears.

The Contessa Gemma Castellani di Monte was an ambitious and a sceptical woman. From her youth up she had always had an ungoverned love of splendor and as she grew older this passion had increased till it had mastered her whole soul. As a girl at school she had always made friends with the richest and grandest of her companions, scorning those whose mothers were not elegantly dressed, or who came without a carriage and servants in livery. As she grew up her one dream was a rich husband and a title, and this desire so filled her heart that it was incapable of any other sentiment. She laughed at love. If she

heard of a married couple so devoted that they
withdrew from society the better to enjoy each
other's company, she laughed them to scorn :
" Everyone to their taste !" was all she had to say
to them ; and all she asked with regard to the
married pair was the amount of their income and
of the wife's settlement; whether she dressed well,
if they received much company or went out much,
if they had a good carriage and how many horses
they kept. In the innermost depths of her heart
her fondest desire was to ride on horseback in a
long flowing habit; but she was one of a numerous
family and her father, who was a banker, could not
give her more than a hundred thousand francs
without doing injury to his business. Her mother
had explained to her very clearly that with so
modest a dowry she must not give herself too
many airs, or she would scare any possible suitor ;
and handsome Gemma, to whom no fate seemed
more horrible than that of remaining an old maid,
had kept her ambitions as to a riding-horse to herself, fully intending, however, to impress them on
her husband as soon as she had secured him. But
she counted largely on her beauty and was quite
resolved not to sacrifice her ambitious dreams to

any of the young stock-brokers who offered her their hearts and a share of their slender fortunes— lawyers and small land-owners.

One day, when she was visiting at the house of one of her grand acquaintance, a gentleman was introduced to her, a retired general; with a title, about thirty hairs on the whole of his head, and sixty years on his shoulders. Some well-informed person let out also that he was a millionaire and the fair Gemma soon confided to the mistress of the house: "That no young man that she had seen had ever impressed her so favorably as this noble looking man with his intellectual brow. And after all he was not old—she did not believe that he was more than fifty : certainly he did not look it ; and at fifty a man is in the prime of life. She, to be sure, was hardly nineteen, but she was sure that if he were to ask her to marry him she would make no difficulties; a husband was the better for having had a long experience of life, and a safer guide for a young wife. She, for her part, could not understand how a woman could entrust her future fate and happiness in the hands of a thought-less youth. . ."

She knew what she was doing and to whom

she was speaking, did the fair Gemma. Her con-
fidante did not fail to repeat her speech to the
millionaire general; then she reported to the
young lady the count's appreciation and gratitude
—how glad he should be to win so handsome and
so reasonable a wife; but at his age he could not
venture — he should fear to seem ridiculous. . .

" Of course, I know that he never thought of
such a thing!" said Gemma. " But I have thought
of it; though I have never hoped for such good
fortune. Papa, I know, has some rich banker in his
eye, some younger man — and I shall marry him
no doubt: but if this respectable gentleman had
offered himself I should have accepted him with
greater confidence. . ."

The go-between friend again took care to repeat the girl's encouraging sentiments, and at the
end of a couple of months the banker's daughter
became a countess and the mistress of a fine fortune; and one of the bridegroom's gifts was a
saddle-horse.

The first seven years of her married life flew
with giddy swiftness; the Countess Gemma rushed
about with delirious hurry from pleasure to
pleasure; dress, amusements of every kind, sump-

tuous entertainments at home, on which she spent
in an evening the income of a twelve-month, and
gay excursions into the country had turned her
brain. She was very soon accustomed to her title,
but still she liked to hear it; she was never tired of
compliments to her beauty, and her elegance, and
admiration, however extravagant, never satiated
her. At first her husband, taking her at her word
as to his mission to guide his young wife, had tried
to keep this wild excitability in check; but the
only result had been endless squabbling which had
enhanced the countess's appreciation of the
pleasures she could only win by a pitched battle ;
and at length the general had resigned himself to
his lot of being his wife's guardian in the literal
sense of escorting her wherever she chose to seek
satisfaction for her vanity or love of amusement.
In the summer, at Baden or at Vichy, in the gay
world of Paris or of London, the old officer never
failed to introduce and attend his handsome young
wife.

Fifty thousand francs a year are hardly an am-
ple income on which to live in this style; they
got into debt. They held on as long as they could,
but at last they were obliged to sacrifice almost

everything to their creditors and reduce their mode
of life in some proportion to the narrow income
that was left to them. The countess gave up the
aristocratic society in which she moved; not for
worlds would she have cut a less splendid figure
than before; and she condescended to shine in a
humbler circle, in which she could still make some
show with a carriage with only one horse, and
without any saddle-horses. And thus it happened
that Giovanni had met her in the houses of Signora Berti and her acquaintances.

Flirtations more or less serious had always held
a place in the countess's programme of amusements. But passion had never touched her heart.
Her haughtiness and her love of luxury had always kept would-be lovers in check; and she, on
her part, loved herself too dearly, and was too
much absorbed in making herself talked of as the
most elegant woman in Milan ever to have leisure
of mind or heart for falling in love. Safe in her
beauty and her youth, she needed no arts to win
admiration; and this absence of coquetry with
the haughtiness she derived from her high
opinion of herself, had gained her a reputation
for honesty and had in fact proved her safe-

guard; she was supposed to be as unassailable as a fortress.

Nothing short of the excitement, the ecstasy, the madness, in which Giovanni had spoken that evening, under the influence of his wild struggle with his fervid youth and unsatisfied cravings, could have emboldened him to utter to a woman whose position was so unimpeachable those four words — as hot and as startling as a kiss — "you are too beautiful."

The countess was but eight and twenty, and of love she knew nothing but the half parental affection of her husband of near seventy. The passion that was latent in her soul flamed up at the spark of Giovanni's glance, at the breath of his voice, and she no more thought of resisting their fascination than she had ever thought of resisting any of her other desires. Her egoism was in itself a passion; she could refuse herself nothing. That night when she went home, alone in her room she wept tears of rapture and of rage as she recalled the clasp of Giovanni's hand and the deep glow of his dark eyes. When and where could they meet again? A wide horizon of new delights opened before her, and an unexplored world.

Above the vanity of feeling that she was beautiful and admired, soared more vehement pride of feeling that she was loved — the pride of loving in return.

Giovanni was captivated by this woman. He sought her, followed her, wrapped her in a halo of passion; and when the fading image of Rachel rose before his fancy—no longer like a vision from heaven, but like a statue receding from his view — he would say to soothe his conscience: " A love like this, a passing fever for a married woman, is like a flower plucked by the way. It makes no real difference."

Still, not for worlds would he have renounced the idea of plucking the flower. He went wherever he was sure to meet the countess ; and always kept near enough to gaze at her handsome person. He would seize the opportunities offered by a quadrille to touch her hand, and there was in that grasp an electric current which made their fingers thrill and clasp so tightly that it was anguish to tear them apart, and once parted they quivered to meet again. Giovanni was not a great dancer ; but one evening, finding himself close to the countess as a polka was beginning, he silently bowed and offered her his hand. She took it; he clasped her to his heart as though he would carry her off, as if he could absorb her into his being, breathed on her hair caressed her with his gaze, and as he led her back to her seat, held her hand with a pressure which conveyed an epitome of all the tender and eager devotion which he had kept in subjection during that dance. But he said nothing. He was happy enough in the mere sense of passion that fired his whole being. He felt that she loved him; and that consciousness was enough to intoxicate him; there was something pathetic to him in these speechless joys; he lingered over them and was in no hurry to shorten them by an explanation. He knew that the explanation must come, and dreamed of it as a crowning joy; but he wanted it to come from her, letting her go on from one sweet phase to the next, and dreading lest, if he hastened to an end, he might lose that fragrance of sentiment, or one of the wordless and playful details of their passion which made it so exquisite.

Still, he foresaw the end.—How, when, where? He knew not; but he was sure of it and that was enough.

CHAPTER XXIV.

ONE day Giovanni had a note from Signora Berti, begging him to go to see her because she wished particularly to introduce him privately to a friend of hers. He found her in her drawing-room with the wife of Signor Ipsilonne, a banker who was seriously compromised in an action that was to be tried with regard to certain forgeries. A most unfortunate resemblance between his writing and that of one of the persons implicated, had led to his being indicted; and of two experts employed by the court, one swore that he recognized the banker's writing, while the other only doubted and dared not deny his guilt. In fact he was innocent; his heart-broken wife had begged to be introduced to Giovanni, in the hope that he would conduct his defence with as much zeal and skill as he had displayed in defending the tavern-keeper.

It was a case of great importance and interest which promised to secure him a fresh triumph, and he threw himself heart and soul into the cause of an honest man so fatally implicated in a crime of which he was guiltless. He at once put his time, his brains and his best will at the service of his new client. He smothered his passion, and without wasting time in taking leave of the countess, he rushed off to Naples, to Rome, to Turin, to compare documents, and bring proofs and witnesses in favor of the banker; returning only the day before the trial was to begin. He arrived at Milan by the last train in the evening, after an absence of more than a week. On his table he found a telegraphic message from the parish priest of Fontanetto which had been lying there for some days.

"I grieve to tell you of the death of your father, Doctor Mazza. Found dead in bed this morning. Sanitary regulations require the funeral within twenty-four hours. Telegraph your orders."

Six days ago — the funeral was by this time over and forgotten; it was not long since Giovanni had sent his father a small sum of money, and there was the furniture in the house. It seemed to him that on the whole any instructions from him were now unnecessary and still more his presence at Fontanetto. This was, in fact, quite out of the question with the business of the next day's trial on his hands.

Well, he had done his duty at a great cost to himself, and helped his father in his need; but he could not be a devoted son. The Dottorino's parasitical and intemperate habits, his brutality at home, and the final degradation of *delirium tremens*, to which, as he knew, his father had succumbed, did not invite him to rush about the country to reap the harvest of contempt that was very certainly the sole inheritance the poor wretch had left behind him. He knew that at such a moment he should meet with no consideration; the memory of that ignoble life and squalid death were still too green. On the other hand he did not flatter himself that he, in his own person, could produce any very favorable impression at Fontanetto; and he did not think he was rich enough to renew his claims on Rachel; but the truth was that now the moment had arrived that, five years ago had seemed so remote, he thought it was too soon to think of marrying. So he replied by telegraph that the news had reached him too late and that

he had consequently been prevented attending the
funeral, but that he had every confidence in the
priest, who would no doubt have seen that all was
decently conducted.

Giovanni reflected with deep dejection on the
life of crapulous dissipation that his father had led
for the last thirty years, on his miserable end,
on his whole worthless existence, at once mean
and graceless; he was moved to genuine compassion. The doctor had had talents and power; he
might beyond a doubt have made some mark —
and he came to nothing. He, Giovanni, was his
son; he had perhaps inherited the germs of his
father's nature; base passions, such as had ruined
his father, lurked perhaps in his heart, only waiting for a moment of weakness or inertia to en-
mesh him and conquer him. He was terrified at
the thought; it revived his devotion to work, his
ambition of glory, his longing to earn an honora-
ble independence; and he spent the night in
studying the great case and preparing his defence.

The trial lasted a week and was a succession
of triumphs for the young advocate. This secured
his fame; every word he spoke now carried

weight and was repeated as authoritative and reported in the papers. The mere fact that he was
to speak filled the court with an audience, and a
crowd of reporters and critics; his sayings were
talked over and commented on, his dicta were
quoted as if they were law by the multitude, and
found due consideration even among persons in
authority. Every evening his table was covered
with visiting-cards and letters of congratulation,
and admiration and friendships were his to command. Still, he could not rid himself of the painful impression left on him by his father's death.
When he went home he felt as though he should
see him lying dead, decrepit before his time, having drunk himself into his grave. He tried not
to think of him, but he could not help it.

Day after day, he saw the countess on the reserved seats in the court, whither she came regularly to hear him. She was dazzlingly beautiful
and splendidly dressed, and attracted all eyes;
bnt she looked at no one but the young pleader.
She was always very early; when he came in she
was always there to receive him. She fixed her
eyes on him — her eyes of a metallic turquoise
blue, and never moved, just catching his glance as

he turned his head, and answering with a respon-
sive flash that went straight to his heart. While
making his defence he addressed himself for the
most part to her; he was eager and agitated, and
felt the need of a friend's presence. She was always in the same place and the same attitude, her
eye riveted on him as if it were held by a mag-
netic force. Then her violet orbs were dimmed and
clouded; there were tears in them; but she did
not cover her eyes with her handkerchief or her
hand; she felt the slow tears roll down her cheeks,
and they trembled on her chin falling like large
beads on her grey silk dress where they spread in
lead-colored circles. Giovanni was greatly touched
by this gaze and these tears, by this spell-bound
beauty, and this overpowering love which defied
all the proprieties to confess itself to him. In
the saddened mood of those days he loved the
countess with the tender attachment of a betrothed ·
lover. He no longer suffered from the frenzied
passion of a month before; he no longer felt that
mad desire to hold her in his arms and clutch her
to his heart, and kiss or eat that rose-tinted snow.
No, he would have been happiest sitting by her
side in mystical rapture, and could have wept on

her bosom. Every day he made up his mind to
go to see her ; but he always put it off. This post-
ponement had a charm in the very intensity of his
craving to be with her; and he never ceased to
think of her.

CHAPTER XXV.

THE Dottorino had sunk into a state of such
complete imbecility that he had glided out of
drunkenness into death probably without knowing
it, and certainly without either crying out for help
or making any attempt to help himself. La Matta
had found him cold in his bed, and had run off to
call the priest who had sent her to fetch the post-
master that he might at once go to Borgomanero
and dispatch the telegraphic message.

"It is to Signor Giovanni," La Matta had said
to the man; she was in such a state of excitement
at the idea of seeing Giovanni again that she had
no thoughts for the tragedy that had happened in
the house. She stood at the door of the baker's

shop muttering to herself quite softly, as if she
were afraid of waking some one:

" The master is dead.   He died drunk." And
she looked quite astonished, for it seemed to her
that she was hearing instead of telling the news.
And when the people in the shop had a little got
over their surprise, she went on, grinning with delight, as if years had already gone by since the
sudden news had burst upon them and there were
no connection between that catastrophe and the
joyful consequences: " Signor Giovanni is the
master now; I shall have to do for him."

In the evening the priest, seeing that Giovanni
neither came nor telegraphed, said that the body
must be buried.   La Matta was petrified.   She
gazed at the dead man, whose mouth was a little
on one side as if he were mocking her as he lay
in his coffin, and she realized that he was leaving
her.   Then she thought of the unknown remote-
ness of her young master and she began to cry,
wailing piteously: " Oh, however shall I find him ?
What shall I do ?"

It had always been the poor soul's ideal of life
that she should serve Giovanni, and live with him.
In the devotion of her slave-like affection she had

never dreamed of anything but to serve him ; but
that she had longed for with an intensity that had
made it the only aim and end of life to her on earth ;
and even when, in church, she vaguely dreamed
of the joys of paradise she still thought of Giovanni above her and herself at his feet in a state
of beatitude to which she would never have as-
pired in this sphere, but which seemed to her the
perfection of bliss in heaven.   For the present
she indulged in less celestial delights.   She would
sit for hours wrapped in visions of dinners she
would prepare for Giovanni ; she knew that he
was fond of *Risotto** and she pictured the whole
process of cooking a superlative *Risotto ;* she
added mushrooms, and even truffles ; and she
laughed to herself with glee as she fancied him
eating it and saying :   " What a good Risotto !"

She got the priest's and the chemist's cooks to
teach her a number of elaborate concoctions on
which to feed her dreams of devotion.

But where was he — this master to whom she
was ready to give her heart's blood ?   Where was
she to find him ?   Suppose she was to lose herself

* A dish of rice with grated cheese, and tomato, or gravy with
saffron.

on the way? And even the dead master was leaving her—she had not loved him but she had taken good care of him because he was her Giovanni's father, and because she had an ill-defined sense of that old drunkard being in some way a tie between her and the absent lad.

The dead man was buried, and when La Matta came home from standing by his grave, her face all swollen by long and desperate weeping, she found the priest, who had got back before her, in the house displaying the furniture and other possessions of the deceased to his creditors. The doctor had spent all the money sent him by his son at the tavern, the inn parlor and the tobacconist's, and he had left debts at almost every shop in the place, besides owing arrears of rent.

"The debts amount to four hundred francs in all," said the priest. "And then there is the funeral, and the church dues . . . it is no use to count on the son, for he has not even answered nor come; but by selling the furniture we shall realize a small sum which may perhaps pay everything."

La Matta, who had stood listening open-mouthed, turned pale and began to tremble.

What! sell the furniture! That furniture among
which she had dreamed of ending her days with
Giovanni! His bed — the table on which she had
so fondly hoped to lay his dinner. Those books
he had always prized so much! She stood in
silence, absorbed in elaborate calculations, paying
no further heed to what the others were saying
about a friendly sale, and legal expenses, and
things that she did not understand. Then going
away she ran to open her money-box and taking
out her savings-bank book she carried it to the
priest, laughing with delight, though her eyes were
still full of tears.

"What do you want to do with it?" asked the
priest.

"To buy the furniture. . . ." said the poor
soul.

"As a loan to your master's son?"

"It is his," said La Matta with magnanimous
conviction, "and he is the master."

"But what will you do with the furniture?"

"Take it to the master. But you must tell me
where he is."

The good man was perplexed; he did not wish
to take advantage of the poor servant's ignorant

generosity; on the other hand he knew that the furniture could not fetch more than a hundred francs or so. The five hundred francs that La Matta had to offer were enough to pay all the creditors and the parish dues as well. He thought the matter over for a long time, for his mind was not a rapid one; but he came to a conclusion at last.

" Well, you shall buy the furniture as a commission from the avvocato, and you shall lend him the rest of your savings to pay his father's debts. I will see that you have enough left to pay for your journey and the carriage of the things; and then you can go to Milan with them and tell him how matters stand and he will make it good to you. You can tell him that if he does not take your word for it he can write to me, and I will be your witness that you have lent him five hundred francs. . . . "

Of all this La Matta did not understand a word; she was wholly absorbed in the idea of going to Milan to find Giovanni, and taking him his furniture which he would be so delighted to have. As to where Milan might be, or how she was to get there, she thought no more about it. The priest would tell her the way. She was going to "do for" Giovanni, to cook his dinner, to brush his clothes, to make his bed. How she would shake up the maize in the mattress so as to make it thick and comfortable. He did not know how elastic a bed could be made. She kept saying to the neighbors:

"He will want for nothing now poor boy. I am going to look after him." And she said it with the profoundest pity, with a feeling of his long destitution, as though, since he had been away from her, no one could have done him those services and he had remained in utter abandonment, waiting till she should come. She was transfigured by happiness. She took leave of everybody saying: "You will see me no more."

But she uttered the words of eternal farewell with a chuckle of satisfaction; she could never cease laughing and the smile on her face had become a spasmodic grin and convulsion of joy. She spent several days and even nights in cleaning, wrapping and packing, always with her thoughts vaguely wandering round the visions she had so long indulged of the dishes she should cook for Giovanni, of his shoes tucked under her

arm and polished!—polished till they were as
bright as a looking-glass and her shoulders ached
for the rest of the day.

Her departure from Fontanetto in the cart, and
even the railway—which she saw for the first time
at Novara—did not disturb her absorbed imaginings. She watched the porters with dismay as
they carried off her precious goods to the luggage
vans, far away from the third-class carriage into
which the guard who looked at her ticket desired
her to mount, and she ran off towards the goods
vans to travel in one of them with her cherished
charge. It took a volume of explanations to make
her understand and return to her place. She looked
suspiciously at the scrap of card which was to en-
title her to recover her property at Milan and held
it tightly clutched though she had no faith in its
efficacy.

The guard said persuasively: "You will see
how fast you go and how soon you get there.—
Jump in." But she would not give way.

"Are you sure," she said, "that they will
give them back to me when I get to Milan."

She hardly noticed the swiftness of the pace;
it could not possibly be rapid enough for her de-

sires. When she got out at Milan she flew at the first porter she saw, and cared for nothing but the restitution of her furniture. The man who carried the bales, seeing this species of savage, asked her: "Is it the first time you have been in Milan?"

La Matta anxiously put out her hand to protect a rickety chest of drawers that he was lifting and made no reply.

"You will see what a fine large place it is," the man went on; "a bigger place than your town. Where have you come from?"

"Mind you do not break it; set it down very gently," cried La Matta, entirely absorbed in her anxieties for the chest of drawers.

She marched through the streets behind two trucks drawn by the porters, never taking her eyes off her property and thinking of nothing else. In the square in front of the cathedral the conversational porter turned round to enjoy her astonishment. But La Matta was not thinking of the cathedral. All she thought of was that she was going to see Giovanni, to stand before him, to take him by surprise; and her heart beat wildly with an unaccountable dread. Then she thought of his delight at seeing his furniture.

"All those blessings, those beautiful things that they were going to sell!"

The porter called out to her: "Look up, I say look up; it is finer than San Gaudenzio at Novara."

La Matta looked up; she beheld a huge white mass with an image of the virgin at the top. She crossed herself, and then she walked on again with her eyes on the trucks.

"What idiots these country louts are," growled the man; and he gave the truck a heavy jolt by way of revenge.

CHAPTER XXVI.

LA MATTA had a note, given her by the priest, with Giovanni's address; *Via del Capuccio.* She would not give it up to the porter but showed it anxiously to two or three passers-by asking: "Where is it? Which way do I go?" And she had pretended to direct the men as to the road. Of course it was they, in reality, who guided her, and they drew up at the door which, as she could not read, she would not have known otherwise. Giovanni was not at home. His clerk opened the door and stood in dismay at seeing the peasant-woman followed by two men loaded with old furniture.

The young lawyer had but three rooms: his office, a sitting-room, and his bedroom. The clerk hesitated to allow the rooms to be crowded up with this lumber, but La Matta stared at him with an air of steady defiance saying:

" This is his furniture, and I am his servant."

The porters, on the other hand, were growling that they could not stand there to all eternity with those loads on their heads. He was forced to let them put down their burdens — one, two, three— till the trucks were unloaded. There was a crate on the writing-table, and the old empty book-case, set up in front of the wardrobe in the bedroom, hid the looking-glass; the packing case that held the books filled up the bay of the window, and the rooms were filled with halt and lame chairs, mattresses rolled into bales, and sideboards.

La Matta contemplated the furniture of the modest lodgings, lost in admiration; she thought it splendid. " Still, it is not his own," she thought.

She had a confused remembrance of having heard, when Giovanni first went to college, that he would not need to take a bed or other furniture, because he would live in furnished rooms.

"They are much better than his," she owned to herself, as she examined the iron bedstead, and the arm-chair covered with cheap worsted damask, "but they are too handsome, they are too much to think about. He cannot take a run and leap over that little table, all polished as it is ; he would leave the mark of his feet on it. . . ."

And perfectly consoled by her recollections of Giovanni's games as a boy, she smiled affectionately at the old table that encumbered the passage.

" He will feel more at home with the things he knows so well. . . ." And she fancied his greeting them as old friends ; he would look at them one by one, and laugh with glee over the recollections they would bring to his mind, and almost caress them ; and tell her how glad he was to have them again, and how well she had done to bring them to him, and what a pity it would have been to sell them, and rub his hands and jump for pleasure and say :

"Now I shall feel at home, and we shall be so comfortable!"

She was excited in picturing to herself the handsome lad that she had parted from five years since; and she fancied him as all the happier for the gift that she had brought him.

Then she studied his clothes, which hung from a row of pegs, turning them round and over and furtively slipping her hand into the sleeve of a coat; then she smiled and exclaimed aloud:

"Why it is silk!"

Near the bed stood an arm-chair, and on the rug was a slipper, sole uppermost. She picked it up, found the fellow under the bed and placed them side by side. She patted and stroked the dirty chair-back, passing her hand lightly over the seat; her heart was full, and yielding to an irresistible impulse, after glancing round her as though she feared to be detected in the act, she sat down on the edge—the very edge, of the chair in which he was wont to sit. A sort of intoxication came over her; she trembled from head to foot; and at last she gave herself up to a silent and soothing fit of tears.

Presently the bell rang; La Matta started to

her feet and rushed to the door. It was he of course, come home, and she was there — his servant, to receive him, to wait upon him. How glad he would be to find her there! Her heart was bursting with tender delight. She glanced at the old bed in the corner of the room and then at the door, and her eyes sparkled like fire ; perhaps she was thinking that she might look at him asleep through the key-hole, as she used to do at Fontanetto.

She heard the clerk open the door and then a sweet deep voice, as full as church music, exclaimed in tones of the utmost astonishment:

"What is all this?"

"A peasant woman is come . . . a servant of yours," replied the clerk.

La Matta had gone through a spasm of agitation at the sound of that voice; she gulped down a sob that seemed like to choke her and rushed into the sitting-room crying:

"It is I, Signor Giovanni, it is La Matta!" And stooping with her clasped hands between her knees she stood looking at him, rocking herself backwards and forwards and laughing till the tears ran down her cheeks.

"Oh, it is you, my poor girl! And how are you?" said Giovanni heartily.

La Matta could only answer by laughing again; the lump in her throat prevented her speaking.

"I am very glad to see you," added the young man, clapping her on the shoulder. "Very glad." And this time the choking found relief in a sob, and the poor woman hid her face in the corners of the shawl that she wore over her head and knotted under her chin. "There, there," said Giovanni kindly," do not agitate yourself. Sit down; rest yourself. We will talk by-and-bye." And he went into his bedroom.

But he soon came out again, stood for a moment in the door-way to make sure that she had got over her first emotions and then said:

"Well, and how did you manage to bring all these things?"

"They are yours," replied La Matta, and her face beamed with delight at being able to give him this splendid assurance.

"And you have made the journey here on purpose to bring them?" asked Giovanni, without any of that rapture which La Matta had expected.

"It was very good of you, and I am very much obliged."

La Matta repeated: "They are your own."

"And are there no debts to pay?"

"No; everything is paid."

Giovanni had sent enough money to his father to believe very readily that the deceased doctor had left no debts, and perhaps enough to discharge the funeral expenses.   He made a tour of the room, looking at the crate on the writing-table, and two bed-posts against a bureau; absently moving an old salt-box that was standing on the clerk's desk; then he turned again to La Matta and repeated his thanks.

"You are really too good; you need not have taken the trouble to come all this way for the sake of this rubbish.   It might have been sold down there — or you might have kept it all."

"Oh! but they are yours," the poor soul said for the third time, with a tightening pain at her heart.

"What of that?" said Giovanni; "I would have given them to you with pleasure in return for your care of the poor old man."

La Matta felt as if the blood were freezing in

her veins; this was not the welcome she had expected; she felt as if she were being turned out of
doors, and quailed at the thought of finding herself alone in the world. Giovanni, seeing her
stand abashed and speechless, fancied he understood, and went on :

"But I daresay you did not know where to
to put all the things; of course you could not
take them with you to a new place. Where are
you going now ?" And he asked with genuine interest : " Have you found a situation ?"

This was like a pistol-shot in the hapless
woman's heart. He did not want her then! It
had never occurred to him to keep her with him!
The shock was so great that she sank on to a chair
and began to cry and wail :

"Oh me! oh me! oh, I am a miserable
woman !" Giovanni sat down by her and tried to
comfort her.

"Do not distress yourself so much. If you
have not got a place I will try to find you one ;
meanwhile you can stay here a few days and I
will give you money enough to live with your fos-
ter mother till you find a comfortable situation. You
are not alone in the world you know. I owe much

to you and am most willing to acknowledge it. . ."
He walked up and down the room, a good deal
bored by her presence there; then looking at the
clock and seeing that it was nearly six, he went
on: "But you must be hungry. I always dine at
a restaurant and have nothing here to offer you. I
will send my clerk with you to an inn near this
where you can get some dinner and a bed. You
can stop there two or three days till I see what is
to be done. They are very good people, and the
children will take you about to see the sights.

La Matta did not stir. She had pulled her
kerchief down over her forehead and sat mute
with her head bent.

"Will you come? or what do you mean to
do?" asked Giovanni a little out of patience. She
felt that she must make some answer; with a great
effort she stammered out: "I do not know."

He was accustomed to this declaration of
ignorance from the poor simple creature; but at
this instant, seeing her refuse to eat or sleep
when she was so much in need of food and rest,
it struck him that she must lack money, so, opening the drawer of his table, he took out a hundred-
franc note and put it into her hand saying:

"There, take that. It is for you and I will pay all your expenses at the inn, and your journey when you want to go home. And if at any time you want help you have only to get some one to write to me, for you have always been thoroughly good and faithful, and I will never lose sight of you."

This was like pronouncing her sentence. He did not mean to keep her with him — it was all over; there was no hope now! The one dream of her wretched life was vanishing and her slave-like devotion was rejected! In this utter ruin of her hopes it seemed to La Matta that the world was crumbling into dust and that she was left standing alone in the midst of a desert. An image formed itself in her mind of the miller's donkey, which spent its life in trotting round a post to turn the mill, and when it was old and could trot no more was taken to Borgomanero and sold for a few francs. She, thought she, was like that donkey.

She dragged herself up and tottered down the stairs; Giovanni followed her. He was really grieved for the poor creature. He himself conducted her to a humble inn where, in former days, he had been wont to eat his modest dinner at a franc a day, and he recommended her to the special care of the hostess. Then, taking her hand with as much respect as if she had been a lady:

"You are tired, poor girl," he said. "Now eat a good dinner and drink a half a bottle of good wine, and then go to bed. Good-bye; do not be out of heart. Come and see me again before you go; and if you ever want me, remember to let me know."

And he went away disturbed and deeply moved. La Matta's appearance on the scene had revived in his mind many vague and distant images of the past; among them his romantic first love, now smothered by the passion that was consuming him. That love was to be the love of the future, of the coming time of peace, rest, and ease. Now — now — his soul was tempest-tossed. During these last few days the countess had magnetized him, subjugated him, with her long, fixed gaze; those eyes had at times pierced his heart to the point of making his voice shake and sobs rise in · his throat; they had told him again and again, with their limpid blue, that she loved him and was wholly his. He was conquered and he knew it; he could no longer live away from her; he had

tried every note of the prelude to their mutual
declaration and was in that state of mind which is
rapture or death. But there was no obstacle —
they might speak and not die.

CHAPTER XXVII.

NEXT morning he had had his father's old furniture cleared out of his office; he desired the
clerk to see that it was stowed in the cellar, and
to unpack the books.

He felt something in the air; he wished his
lodgings had been handsomer. He did not dare
imagine that the countess would come there; but
he expected her to give some sign; he was sure
that they would meet; he must go to her and tell
her that he loved her. But still he hoped that she
would write first. He sat down at his desk; but
he was feverishly impatient. Every time the bell
rang he looked eagerly at the door; and if there
was any delay he called out to the clerk: " Well,
what is it?"

Once the man said :

"It is the chamber-maid from the inn."

"Very good, pay her bill."

But in a minute the clerk came back and said that the woman wanted to speak to him. Giovanni nodded that she might come in and looked up to invite her speak. She shook her head and said solemnly :

"Poor soul, she was like a mad creature."

"Like a mad creature ! Why ?"

"I do not know. She would not say a word. She crouched away in a corner of the parlor and there she stayed all the evening with her eyes fixed as if she had seen a ghost. She howled like a mad dog, and tore her forehead with her nails."

"But what ailed her ?" asked Giovanni.

"Lord knows ! I asked her all manner of questions and so did the mis'es. She did not answer a word but shoved her away and shrieked louder than ever. It was as much as we could do to get her to move when it was time to shut up ; and we heard her sobbing and groaning all night. This morning the mis'es found her still squatting on the floor ; she had never been to bed. She said she wanted to go home and we were only too glad. We had to put her into the omnibus and take her to the station for the first train to Novara. She did not even know how to take her ticket; we took it for her."

Giovanni was puzzled; he had listened rather vaguely, still he took an interest in the poor soul; he said in an undertone:

"What on earth could have ailed her? But I know that the hill country folks cannot bear to be away from their native place; and this poor woman had never been a mile away in her life. She was bewildered and frightened. . ."

Before the chamber-maid had fairly gone the bell rang again and a note was brought in to Giovanni. It was from the countess. He started up and took it into his own hand to read; he thought no more of La Matta.

The Countess Gemma, whose one idea was to indulge her fancies at any cost, had given herself up to her passion without an hour's hesitation. Nay, she had encouraged it by the dreams of a heated imagination; still she always dreamed of a morrow — each day she had said to herself: "To-morrow," picturing the moment when Giovanni

should on his part confess his love—"to-morrow,"
and again "to-morrow."

But as the days went on in slow monotony and
brought no crisis in her romance she felt her heart
tighten with apprehension: "If I should never
see him again!—If he did not love me after all!—
If that evening he only yielded to a transient impulse, and has forgotten it as a man forgets a
drunken fit!"

She felt that she had missed something that
was strangely precious to her, that was necessary
to her very existence. She wanted above all things
that that passion — that intoxication — that delirium—should survive or be revived in Giovanni;
and she had set to work to seek him in the houses
he most frequented, at theatres and balls, dressing
herself in the most bewitching way she could
think of if only she might renew the bliss of that
moment which seemed to have eluded her forever. This pursuit left her weary and nervous;
she would fall into agonies of tears or fits of rage
scolding her maid, tearing her muslins and laces,
or writing desperate letters which she destroyed as
soon as they were written.

At last she heard that he was engaged in a

case of great importance, and had rushed to secure the most prominent place on the reserved benches; she had made a display of her feelings when he spoke and had gloried in this madness which was new to her frivolous nature and supplied the missing note of romance in her life.   All through the trial she had watched the young lawyer with those metallic blue eyes, and exercised all the powers of her will to command his response. She had seen him color and turn pale, thrill and tremble under her gaze, and once more she had triumphed in the belief that he loved her.   Still the days went by and Giovanni did not come.

On returning from the court on the last day of the trial, burning with enthusiasm and admiration for the young hero of the appealing voice, who had drawn tears and applause from all present, the countess had lost all womanly reserve and dignity. She had written with feverish haste:

"Why do you not come to me ?   Do you not know that I love you ?"

This note fired Giovanni's blood, and after the hard work and patient care he had given to this case he rushed madly into the treacherous delights that offered themselves for his acceptance.

It was about eleven in the forenoon. He flew
to the countess unmindful of the hour, of eti-
quette, of everything. He was shown into the
dining-room where the count and his wife were at
breakfast. Giovanni stood stupidly like a man who
is suddenly aroused from a beautiful dream. He
felt it impossible that this lady — who sat eating
a beef-steak and talking small gossip with that el-
derly husband—should be the heroine of romance
who had written to him : " I love you."

In an instant all his intoxicating visions had
vanished ; he felt as though he must have been
acting in delirium, as if nothing was real ; that he
had never been other to this lady than he was at
this minute in her husband's presence. The very
atmosphere, full of the smell of food — this conjugal tête-à-tête — the napkin-rings, each with its
owner's name on it — the table linen, all marked
with their joint initials — the thousand small, common possessions that constituted a visible tie
between them — all these things were outside and
beside protestations of passion, and they suffocated
him. For a moment he fancied that her note had
been a ruse to make him pay a call that had long
been due, or perhaps to turn the tables on him for

that moment of aberration when he had breathed the words: "You are too fair!"

He had to join them at breakfast, scarcely capable of understanding the questions they put to him as to the details of the trial, but answering at considerable length, as though he were trying to justify his intrusion at such an hour by affecting to have called on purpose to give the general this information. He was excessively embarrassed at finding himself there, and could not imagine how he was to get away again; looking at the countess, and seeing her perfectly cool, smiling and content, he could not believe that she was under the dominion of any violent emotion. He, and he alone was a fool! At last the count rose from the table, shook hands with his visitor and asked his wife's permission to withdraw to smoke a cigar with the air of a man who is accustomed to yield to his wife.

"Gemma cannot endure the smell of tobacco in the house," he explained and he went.

The very air of the room seemed to have grown rarer as he left it; all the prose of the situation had gone with him. The countess, who was opposite the door which he had gone out,

seemed transfigured ; her turquoise eyes sparkled
with a flash as keen as points of steel, and she
trembled visibly.

Giovanni rose and went towards her but he
did not speak.   The commonplace of politeness
was no longer possible between them.   They understood each other too well, and clasped hands
without a word.   Giovanni drew her to him, and
the countess, bowing her head on his breast, burst
into a convulsive fit of weeping.

From that day the Countess Gemma and Giovanni were inseparable.   Wherever she went he
was certain to appear, and at her own dinners and
evening parties the young lawyer was as inevita-
bly to be met as if he were one of the family.   It
was difficult to be there before him, or to stay
later.   The countess, on her part, never failed to
be present in court when Giovanni was engaged
in a case ; she was always well informed as to
every trial in which he was concerned, and was as
triumphant when he was successful as if it were a
personal matter.   Her first love, that had found
her at thirty, had taken entire possession of her
with an imperious violence that would brook no
check nor bridle ; she seemed to take a pride in

her dishonor as much as to say to all the world : "This man is my property."

They were as often together as they could contrive to be, and even in the midst of acquaintance could snatch a moment to exchange a word, to touch hands as he gave her a cup of tea or to look over a line in the newspaper together. He gave no more time than was absolutely necessary to his work and she to her household and toilet and the exigencies of society. If business required Giovanni's absence from Milan the countess would leave town when he did, and not reappear in the world till he returned ; she had a friend or a relation to visit in the country—but she did not care whether any one believed it.

There was no end to their follies. They ascended Monte Rosa together, dressed in costumes of the same grey tweed, with ties of the same color, boots by the same maker, hats alike of felt, with an eagle's feather and a white scarf tied round them. On their *alpenstocks*, under the name of the place and the date of their expedition, they cut their initials intertwined, and at every inn they wrote their names side by side like a newly-married couple with a sentimental motto.

On another occasion they went to Monte Carlo, where they lost every franc they had with them, and remained in pawn at the hotel till Giovanni had telegraphed to Milan and received money enough to release them.

The general was perhaps ignorant of his wife's escapades; or perhaps he knew of them and was resigned to fate. However that may have been, they were no secret from the rest of the world. It was one of those scandals that society chose to wink at till it had become accustomed to it; and at length the guilty lovers, having exhausted their round of folly, got used to it too and their affection assumed an almost matrimonial placidity. It was by this time too firmly established and too widely known for any film of romance; it had no halo of mystery, no anxious terrors of discovery. It had made itself a groove and ran smoothly on, fed on little subterfuges and pleasantries rather than on sentiment; and on these terms it had become permanent.

Gemma, however, under the guise of a flirtation still cherished the passion which had come upon her with the fever of a first love, while Giovanni, after yielding to the storm, had found it no more than a sweet habit which was rest after his work and not too exciting, while it brought him none of the torments of jealousy and left his mind at ease. And he was grateful and devoted. From time to time he still remembered his old ambition to grow rich enough to force from old Pedrotti his consent to his marrying Rachel. And now he was rich, he was earning fifty thousand francs a year. But how long it had taken him to reach this point! It was lucky—most lucky—that the young girl had not pledged herself to wait for him. By this time she was married, no doubt, and the mother of a family. Sometimes, when he had had a particularly hard or worrying day, he would sigh and think that he would have liked to be the father of a family, that he was growing old in solitude, and that by-and-bye he would have no one to love him and care for him . . . but then he met the countess, spent a pleasant hour or two with her, and forgot his forebodings.

CHAPTER XXVIII.

YEARS went by, during which Giovanni's fortune, fame, and social position constantly improved. He was no longer young; he was five and thirty, and a man of high consideration; he was at the head of one of the largest lawyers' offices in Milan; he had a splendid set of apartments, was decorated with the cross of St. Maurice and St. Lazarus, and was certain of his seat at the next election. The countess was still handsome, and with the constancy which is peculiar to women, she was still in love. So long as Giovanni was attentive to her and docile to her wishes she still could be happy in a calm affection which brought her nothing but pleasure and amusement.

But a time came at last when, with Giovanni, the little formalities of love-making fell into desuetude. By degrees—unconsciously indeed—Giovanni ceased to appear devoted and let her see too plainly that he was taking a more business-like view of the situation.

"This," he said, "is the private and personal side of my life; it must not interfere with my public career. I have other duties: my office, my business, money-matters and politics. I must read the papers and go to my clubs. When I am free I ask nothing better than to be with you; but I cannot spend the day in dancing attendance on you. . . ."

Gemma had cherished her romance; her dreams were still of an exclusive and eternal passion and she could not resign herself to this change in Giovanni. She tried to find a cause for it, wrote him long pages of lamentation, and when they met she spent the few hours he had to spare, in scenes of recrimination and jealousy. But Giovanni had not really changed at all. He, who had never ceased to love her in a man's way and had even affected a certain effusiveness as their intimacy had increased, could not see what she had to complain of and thought her unjust and exacting.

"At our age," he said, "we cannot give ourselves up to the follies of two young lovers."

This speech had seemed peculiarly cruel to the

countess.   He thought her old then!—She was
in despair.   " There is an end of it then ! That is
why he no longer cares for me."   And she was
half wild with jealousy whenever he spoke to a
woman younger than herself.

On more than one occasion she caused him the
greatest embarrassment by interfering between
him and an imaginary rival.   One evening, when
he was on the point of leading to the piano the
young wife of one of his friends, who was about
to sing, the countess declared that she felt ill and
must go home at once for she was fainting, and
she asked Giovanni to accompany her so that he
was obliged to leave before the lady had sung her
song.   Giovanni complied, but with extreme an-
noyance; and when they were in the carriage he
complained of the ridiculous figure she made him
cut by making such a scene. An angry discussion
resulted which lasted till they reached home, and
was followed by a long fit of sulks, and an exchange of penitent and beseeching letters on the
part of the countess for distant answers from Giovanni, ending in a superficial reconciliation.

And so time still went on between peace and
war; with occasional gleams of happiness to re-

mind them of the past and make them believe
that it could return, and then a revulsion of feeling, fresh differences, gloomy coldness over some
trifle — because Giovanni had bowed to some
other woman, or for some personal slight real or
fancied.

One winter it happened that a lady, a public
singer, having a quarrel with the manager of one
of the theatres, went to consult Signor Mazza, the
great lawyer, and put her cause into his hands.
Giovanni had of course frequent need of seeing her,
to hear her statements and make enquiries. The
singer was a handsome woman and the gossips did
not fail to take advantage of so good an opportunity. The countess was fairly beside herself
with jealousy; she tried to insist on Giovanni's
giving up the case, imploring him to do so as a
proof of his regard for her; but Giovanni would
not give way. In fact he was weary of this false
scheme of life, and day by day felt less inclined to
yield. The countess had but a melancholy carnival; she felt herself eclipsed; and she saw with
anguish that the more she tried to retain her admirer the less hold she had on him, and she vented
her ill-humor in petty aggravations which embit-

tered them both. She would leave the theatre in the middle of the play if Giovanni bowed to his client in the opposite box.

Then Lent came; there was no more play-going, and she had fewer opportunities of watching Giovanni; but whenever he was not by her side or she failed to find him at the house of some common acquaintance she took it for granted that he was in attendance on the singer and no argument could persuade her to the contrary. Giovanni was at length quite out of patience and ceased to trouble himself about her vagaries. Her next step was to institute a perfect persecution of the singer. She got spiteful paragraphs inserted in a theatrical newspaper, and even went the length of writing her anonymous letters, in which she accused her of feigning an imaginary lawsuit in order to establish relations with a certain rich and celebrated pleader.

Giovanni, to whom the lady showed these letters, took it very ill; he was annoyed at the absurd position in which the countess had planted him, and in his wrath he reproached her with much acrimony for so mean an action. This was the crisis. The countess, possessed by her own senseless jealousy, could conceive of no way of recapturing Giovanni but by making him equally jealous. She appeared in society escorted by a young fellow who had for a long time been her humble admirer, and pretended to have put him on a confidential footing of the greatest intimacy. Giovanni saw and was deeply disgusted; but he was not jealous; he did not reproach the fickle fair one for her faithlessness and wrote no despairing remonstrances. His heart had grown cold and so far as she was concerned it remained so.

The countess was desperate out of revenge, or disgust, or vanity, or all three, she resolved on a step so mad that perhaps her only motive was the opportunity it afforded her for writing the following letter:

" I thought more highly of you than you have ever deserved and you were never worthy of my love. So long as you needed my countenance to make your way in the world you pretended to be devoted to me; now you have made a position, and you throw me over like an ungrateful wretch. But you need not fancy that I shall spend the rest of my days in tears of regret; you are not worth it. Some one else still thinks me charming enough to devote his life to me, as you never did, and to defy the opinion of the world which is your idol. Make yourself happy with your new conquest while I try to forget in the affections of a generous man one who never was generous. . ."

By the time this coarse abuse reached Giovanni's hands all Milan was talking of the countess's flight with her young lover. Giovanni was disgusted and outraged; every illusion of his fancy was dispelled and his faith in the dignity of humanity was shaken. There had never, it is true, been the slightest tinge of the ideal in his passion for this woman. He had succumbed to the fascinations of her beauty and elegance; he had come to know her at the most critical period of his manhood, after years of hardship, and when his fancy and his feelings were keenly impressionable from the long patience of a mortified love. He had followed the bent of his youth, and found himself happy or unhappy without ever troubling himself to form an opinion as to her moral qualities, her mind or her character. He knew he could never marry her and had been satisfied to see that she was handsome, brilliant and admired. She was a mistress who did him credit and kept

him in a good humor, but he had never imagined her
to be superior to the other women he might meet.
At the same time his pride would have prevented
his ever dreaming that the woman he had loved
could fall so low; so when he had it brought
home to him he was forced to think ill of all her
sex, unless he could believe that she was in fact
the worst; and though, as he had ceased to love
her, he could feel no personal regrets his life was
the darker and more desolate for her defection.
She had carried away with her the fondest of his
illusions and it was that that he mourned.

He thought to console himself by really making love to the actress; but that lady was too
much accustomed to being made love to, to value
his attentions and as he grew explicit she explained
on her part that she had "a real attachment."

The inference was obvious — if she had not
had this "real attachment" his wealth and position would have been sufficient temptation, though
she would not have affected to care for him. This
was a fresh shock to Giovanni. At his age life

had no new experiences to offer. He had exhausted all the poetical illusions of his youth, then he had seen their folly, had viewed the world from a more practical stand-point, had regarded all his purer sentiments and higher aspirations as childish dreams, and had learnt to throw himself exclusively into the joys and pleasures of life. And now, when he was beginning to see the folly of this view also, he began to think that his earlier errors were on the whole preferable. He recalled with regret the honest enthusiasm that he had formerly felt for the causes he had to defend, the zeal and devotion he had been wont to bring to his work, the nights he had sat through longing for more employment, and the excitement of his investigations. Now, cases poured into his office, but they brought him no pleasure ; he looked them through calmly with the indifference of experience, he defended his clients without eagerness, without passion, sometimes even without feeling the slightest care for their fate.

He had started in life in extreme poverty but with a great love in his heart; and the goal he had set before his eyes was wealth and distinction, but still for the sake of that love. Now, wealth and distinction were his — but the love he had lost on the way.

If indeed, he had flown to claim Rachel as soon as he had achieved a respectable position, he might perhaps have been in time to win her ; but at that time the charms of a city life beckoned him another way; the serene idyl of that innocent affection and the calm joys of a married life could not have satisfied him ; it would have been disturbed by the unfed fires of his youthful passions and the delusive aspirations of his unsatisfied ignorance. His inexperience had craved adventure — well, he had tried it, had his fill of it ; and it had left him satiated and cheated, dissatisfied with himself, distrustful of others, alone and hopeless, his heart dry and dead.

These were the saddest days of his life. As he sat in his pretty chambers, or the still more elegant drawing-rooms where he was always welcome, he thought with regret of the last-maker's loft with its ill-joined partitions. As he rose to speak in court, the centre of a crowd of admirers — reporters and short-hand-writers who hung on his lips — and as he listened to their praises, he remembered his first address, delivered to the

wooden shoes that festooned his room; and he
would willingly have gone back to that time, poor
and unknown as he had been, if he could thus
have recovered his lost hope and faith in the success which, now that he had won it, had no
value.

His sins and errors had not been abnormal,
though he had followed the bent of his inclina-
tions; why should he blame himself—any one
else in his place would have done the same. But
his real grief was that this should ever have' been
the bent of his inclination; too late he saw that
his first path had been the right one, and he
would gladly have returned to it — but it was too
late.

CHAPTER XXIX.

GIOVANNI had an invitation to a ball for the
Tuesday of Easter week, and by sheer force of habit
he went. He had so completely accustomed himself to fashionable life, and was by nature so thoroughly refined and gentlemanly, and so much a

man of the world, that he was quite in his element
in the fine houses and the society of ladies, of men
of mark, of ambassadors, great artists, and men of
rank and culture.   He had for some time given
up dancing, he had never gambled and in fact was
not in any way amused ; still, he felt himself in his
element.   That evening he was even duller than
usual and had stood talking politics for some time
with an old senator.   In the midst of a discussion
on the duty on flour, which happened to be the
question of the day, his interlocutor smiled at some
one in the distance, and a young man came forward to speak to him.

"Let me introduce Count V... one of our most
promising diplomatists," said the old gentleman of
a young man of about five and twenty who made
his bow to Giovanni.   Giovanni murmured some
of the usual phrases: "He was much pleased to
make his acquaintance."

"But our acquaintance is of old standing,"
said the young man.   "We have known each
other these sixteen years, if I mistake not."

Giovanni looked at him curiously, but did not
recognize him.

"I was then no more than eight," the young

fellow went on with a smile, "and when I was invited out to dinner I was put to sit at a side table. . ."

Then Giovanni recollected the name and recognized him as one of his little friends at the castle of Fontanetto.

The whole scene with its rural freshness, its sun and shade, the upper table with the ponderous country wits, the fair young girl, all rose up in his mind as he had seen them on that distant day and he exclaimed, as he grasped his new friend's hand with sincere effusion : " How glad I am to see you ! Very glad indeed !"

And it was quite true. This resurrection of the past was a keen delight. His miserable embarrassment, his indignant resentment of the pompous airs of his patrons, the terror of debasing himself that had made him defiant, all had vanished with the occasion that had given rise to them — with his youth that could never return. That picture of quiet peace rose before him in the tender light shed upon it by his thirty years experience, through the mists of a long period of change and disappointment. He did not see himself there as a boy and in his priestly costume, shy and loutish as he had then been ; but as he was now, respected, well-to-do, and longing for nothing so much as rest. He felt a sudden renewal of love for the patriarchal life of his native province, for its green hills,. for the great castle garden, and the ivy-clad walls that shut it in — all seemed grand and picturesque, and he thought there could be nothing more delightful than to retire there and rest in peace.

He took possession of the young diplomatist and for the rest of the evening he kept him by his side, questioning him about Fontanetto and the people he had left there. His new friend had a large estate in the neighborhood which he went to see every year, so he was well informed.

Signor Pedrotti had died of gout some years since, and Rachel was still living alone in that huge castle. Neither before nor since her father's death would she ever hear a word about marrying. Signor Ichese of Maggiora, now one of the most distinguished architects of Rome, had paid his addresses to her ; and the son of another great landowner had proposed to her, a man whose estates included almost all Fontanetto, and Cavaglio, and Ghemme, and who was so rich that he

was known as the Rothschild of Italy. After that
a famous violin-maker had come to settle in the
neighborhood; he was the son of Tognina the
dairy-woman, and had amassed an enormous fortune in America; and he had offered her his hand
and his heart and his millions and his violins into
the bargain; but the signorina had refused them
all. Some said that she cherished a secret passion,
while some said that she had a religious mania.
Giovanni, in his present frame of mind, accepted
the former solution : Rachel cherished an old flame,
and indeed why should he not conclude that she
had been waiting for him ?   When he left Fontanetto he was certain that she loved him.   At
first she had been reduced to submission by her
father's authority and had not dared to write to
him or make any promises in contravention of the
old man's orders.   But time had brought her
strength to resist; and after refusing one offer of
marriage she had understood that this was always
open to her and that she could remain faithful
to her old love without rebelling openly against
her father.   She was sure of Giovanni and trusted
her lover, and had waited unmarried for his
return.

That evening Giovanni, going home early from the ball, carried back with him to his sumptuous chambers all the poetry of his youth. He went up-stairs singing the old ballad that the secretary's wife used to sing; that he had forgotten for so many years, and that had come back to him with all the other memories of his country home:

" Non mi chiamate più biondina bella,
    Chiamatemi biondina sventurata. . ."

He entered his rooms with a firm step and his head held high, with a bright smile on his face, as if he were returning from his first love-meeting. His ideas, so far, were altogether vague, but he had a general sense of the pleasures of such memories; a vision of green meadows, of utter solitude, and restful peace, in which he abandoned himself to the raptures of an idyllic dream and he smiled round at the vacant rooms as much as to say: "I have found my scrap of paradise; I can afford to laugh at the world." He seated himself in the arm-chair by the bed and began slowly to undress, his mind preoccupied by this new sense of comfort. He cast a loving eye on the few remnants of his father's furniture that he had not sent into the basement allowing each to bring back to his mind some incident, some person, some scene of his past. And in their resurrection from their long oblivion all these memories were bereft of the bitterness that had formerly tainted them. They rose again beautified, like the butterfly which leaves behind it the dingy slimy case of the grub. Giovanni was content to dwell on these touching reminiscences.

When he got into his dressing-gown he took up the book he was just then reading ; it was an account of some famous English trials. But this evening the decisions of the London lawyers had no interest for him. He started up and went to the book-case, and there, standing on tip-toe with his lamp held as high as he could reach, he began to hunt through the top shelf, where he kept works of general literature which were not his usual study. His eye fell on a small volume bound in red morocco which he at once seized as if he had lighted on a lost treasure, and he went back to his seat leaving the book-case open. It was the second edition of *i Promessi Sposi* which he had lent so many years before to Rachel. It was the book which he had sent to ask for at the moment when he was quitting home forever, in the hope of finding between its leaves that note he had so humbly sued for, and which, coming back to him without a word, had brought him instead a crushing disappointment. If only she had given him that promise he would have come to Milan bound by a pledge of honor and he would have thought of nothing but keeping that word at any cost. The instant he could have done so without fear of a rebuff he would have flown to claim his betrothed, and his life would have taken a totally different bent; by this time he would have been married for years and at the head of a family, and have known nothing of that wretched interlude with the countess.

All this flashed through his mind as he turned over the leaves of the book in which he had scribbled some marginal notes, marks of admiration or exclamation, all of which brought some association to his mind. Suddenly, as he turned a page, he found a letter — rather dirty and crumpled, but still sealed in its envelope. He shivered — his heart beat violently and he shuddered from head to foot as if he had seen a ghost. It was Rachel's writing! Here was the letter he had prayed for

so many years ago; here was the promise that
would have changed the whole course of his life.
And then he had not been able to find it.

He opened it in the greatest agitation, his
hands shook and his mind was confused. Was he
not even now living again in that distant past and
awaiting in agonizing suspense the sentence that
was to decide his future? The note was brief:

"I cannot set myself in opposition to my
father to marry you. Forgive me for being so
weak — I am his child — but I will never marry
any one but you. I swear it."

Giovanni sat bewildered and stupefied. He
was perfectly positive that this note had not been
in the book when La Matta had brought it back
to him.

"Oh! that stupid creature," he groaned, "she
took it out in order to pick out the Os in the address and put it back when it was too late!" And
he remembered with frightful accuracy a thousand
circumstances that had escaped his notice at the
time — La Matta's sudden attempt to avoid him
when he went to meet her in his impatience; her
embarrassment and objection to allow him to
carry the book when he had snatched it from her,

and finally, his having found her in his room when he went up, for the last time, to fetch down his trunks. All was clear to him now in the light he had acquired in the course of his long legal practice. He said to himself: " It was then that she replaced the letter in the book !" And he lost himself in reflecting on what trifles our fate depends and in wondering what might have been his lot if, as a mere child, he had not taken it into his head to teach a maid of all work her alphabet.

A whole romance *à la Dickens* passed before his fancy, of innocent love and conjugal joys, of home life and domestic peace, which might have been his but for this trivial incident, and it was like a smile from heaven. He lingered with particular pleasure on certain details of sweet tranquillity and certain scenes of tender joys, devoid of all struggle, all disgrace, all terrors ; and they seemed to him all the more lovely by contrast with the stormy existence that had in fact been his and the base passions that had nauseated him. As he dwelt on these thoughts mere regret faded from his mind; love, faith, and happiness filled it entirely. Had he not learnt this very evening that Rachel had refused every offer of marriage ? Well then. It was of course, as he was glad to think, that she had kept her pledge for his sake; she had waited for him.

And he was free, and loved her better now than he had ever done before. What did it matter that her letter had failed to reach him? That he had not known for so long the extent of her generous constancy? The position was the same as it had always been—postponed for a few years, but in no respect altered. Rachel was kind, and sweet, and intelligent, and she was true, incapable of falsehood. He need never fear a mean or disloyal thought in her.

He sat up half the night thinking of her. She could no longer be quite young; she must be of about the same age as the countess or rather less; and the countess was still charming, still young-looking, and had some years before her. Rachel, like her, was fair; but her features were more regular; he felt certain of finding her handsomer than ever now that she had developed into womanhood. He pictured her to himself a little taller and fuller than at eighteen, with that cordial ease and breadth of manner which are gained by contact with the world. Even as a girl she had had much natural grace, good taste, elegant manners and great intelligence . . . she must be a fascinating woman. And she was an orphan; she would be alone to receive him and do the honors of her castle . . . long since no doubt she had ceased to look for him; how surprised she would be to see him once more! It must be a twilight scene; the *dramatis personae* a well-dressed woman and a man of fashion. He, he thought, would arrive on horseback, raising a cloud of dust, and his lady-love would be watching on a tower like the wife of Marbrouk, *"pour voir s'il reviendra."*

In the midst of these rosy visions he fell asleep and dreamed still of love and poetry.

CHAPTER XXX.

GIOVANNI rose early next morning, all impatience to be off to Fontanetto, to find himself once more in that realm of romance and youthful delight and pure devotion, to give that delightful surprise to the good and faithful woman who had waited for

him so long. But it took several hours to arrange
his business and to give the necessary instructions
to his clerks so that they might carry on his affairs during his absence; he could not get away
till the afternoon. How long would he be away?
He did not know, he would not decide. He was
going to find such happiness that he wanted to
feel at liberty to give himself up to it without
measure or stint of time, and without troubling
himself with business.

When he reached Novara he had to wait about
an hour for the first train to Borgomanero. He
remembered how splendid he had once thought
the café of the station. The spring was the fashionable season at Novara; the little town was
talked of at Fontanetto as a realm of bliss. The
visitors who came from thence would talk of the
luxurious fittings of this refreshment room, the
gilt cornices and mirrors, the sofas covered with
velvet, the white marble tables and the magnificent buffet loaded with every luxury; and they
would give rapturous descriptions of the elegance
of the ladies who in summer afternoons sat out in
the gardens, to hear a band play and sip ices. But
now, as Giovanni went into the stuffy little saloon

he felt half suffocated; it had never been cleaned
or decorated since the day when it was opened.
The velvet seats were faded and had lost their pile
till they were as bald as an old man; the gilt cornices tarnished and rubbed in spite of their
shrouds of yellow gauze; on the mirrors thousands
of generations of flies had left their traces, and
you saw your face in them all covered with black
spots; the marble of the tables was scrawled over
with vulgar outlines or mottoes. It was a wreck;
indeed it was not long after enlarged and refur-
nished to make it a little more comfortable.

Behind the counter stood a damsel to whom
two swains of mature years, and of hybrid race
between the fashionable dandy and the country
bumpkin, were paying compliments that she took
as her natural perquisites. She was very upright
and stiff with a waist so tightly laced that she
seemed hardly able to breathe, and her head,
decorated with an elaborate structure of hair, very
smooth and shining, presided over the counter
between two pyramids of biscuit-tins that served
to decorate the marble slab. Outside, an organ
now struck up a polka, and the damsel of the
counter, with that passion for dancing that charac-

terizes the provincial Italian, ran to fetch another girl out of the kitchen and went forth to dance under the portico of the station, deserting her admirers and laughing saucily with her companion at the rather bold remarks they made on her personal appearance.

Presently some of the natives appeared on the scene; the young girls walking first in light dresses and hats in the most extravagant fashion; papa and mamma bring up the rear. There were a few youthful brides in the most gorgeous attire and dazzling jewelry, displaying the latest modes with even greater extravagance than their unmarried sisters. Finally a limited number of dandies who waved a hand at the smart lady of the counter but dared not lift their hats for fear of being identified by the duennas.

This to be sure was not the élite of Novara society; the rank and file rather; but it was the company of which Fontanetto talked, speaking of Novara as in some village in Brittany they might talk of Paris. Giovanni looked on at this provincial scene of dissipation and smiled at his youthful impressions of its splendor; then he fell into a commonplace vein of reflections: " In pro-

portion as we gain in rapture and attain to ease
and luxury and all the pleasures of wealth, life
becomes in fact more difficult, because we feel it
painful to be for a time in a less refined atmosphere than that we are accustomed to ; everything
looks mean, ridiculous or vulgar, whether rightly
or wrongly, and thus we are content . . . At this
moment, what the better am I for being rich ? I
have a sense of being ill at ease under circumstances in which formerly I would have been am-
ply satisfied. . ."

By this time the train was starting and so the
sermon was happily interrupted. Giovanni took
a coupé that he might be alone, he stretched his
legs on the seat and fixing his eyes on the verdur-
ous landscape that unrolled itself before the opposite window he gave himself up to thoughts of
Rachel, of his visit, of their meeting. He recollected perfectly the handsome plan of the house ;
the vast rooms, with their lofty ceilings and cornices with bas-reliefs and ponderous fittings.
Rachel who had received an elegant education had
no doubt taken care to keep up its antique character.

But she herself was modern and had probably

made herself some more fitting nook or bower.
He pictured her to himself in a pretty boudoir
with light furniture — low cosy sofas, rocking-
chairs, turkish cushions, inlaid tables, a pianoforte, a work-table loaded with trifles and flowers,
a few antique hangings gracefully draped over the
wall, little terra-cotta statuettes, china jars on
brackets, a tiger's skin, and a writing-table
with a thousand little instruments of artistic form
and workmanship — a bronze inkstand, paper-
knife, letter-weight, pen-rack — all the costly toys
which certify to their owner's taste Books too,
the modern works that an intelligent woman orders of her bookseller the day they appear. And
flowers everywhere ; on the tables, on the brackets,
in the decorative jardinières in the windows, wherever they could find standing room. And in the
midst of all this simple and tasteful elegance he
saw Rachel, dressed in a black or dark dress cut
with the exquisite skill of some famous modiste ;
one of those dresses that display the figure without tightening it, that are an adornment without
gaudiness, that leave every limb free to move.
With such a fortune as hers she could have no
difficulty in procuring all the refinements of town

life; living in this remote retreat she would have escaped the pretentiousness, the narrowness and the absurdities of provincial fine-ladyism.

He himself knew a woman who had been living for some years in a country-house of her own, and she was one of the most charming women of his acquaintance. She was always to be found in a conservatory which she had arranged as her sitting-room. A large window formed one wall of this boudoir, affording a wide view of the open country with the rocky cliffs of the lake of Lecco on the horizon. The other sides of the room were built over with rock-work and overgrown with ferns, lycopodium, ivy, and other evergreen creepers; producing the effect of a natural grotto which, by being warmed and shut in, was comfortable even during the winter. Next to this bower was the drawing-room and there this lady lived in elegant retirement, among her flowers, with music and books, rarely admitting a few favored intimates, writing letters full of spirit and wit and spending her evenings with a small circle of friends, or not unfrequently one only, who were well content to come out from Milan expressly to see her. She was happy without theatres or entertainments of any kind. Her conversation was always high in tone and taste, because it had no taint of personality. All the time that she saved from visiting and shopping she was free to devote to reading, music, and drawing, and her isolation gave her a certain independence of the prejudices and conventionalities of society which made her superior to the ordinary run of women.

Thus it was that Giovanni pictured Rachel; and he thought to himself that, though he must take her with him to Milan — which he could not leave on account of his business — he would not allow her to make acquaintance with any but the choicest of womankind, whose education was refined and whose reputation was immaculate. And as he called to mind this and that great lady who was always ready to welcome him in her circle, he liked to think that his wife might figure in that sphere of the elect and be their equal or even their superior.

CHAPTER XXXI.

At Borgomanero he took a carriage to drive
to Fontanetto. It was Sunday and he reached the
village during vespers. The street was deserted;
the castle loomed in the distance with its gloomy
walls and dark moat. It was the only object in
scene which impressed him with the solemnity
that he had attributed to it; it was a lordly dwel-
ling fit for its fair mistress. All the windows were
wide open to admit the sweet spring air, but no
one was to be seen at them; not a soul was stirring; it seemed deserted. When Giovanni got
out of the vehicle, chill and pale with excitement,
and knocked at the gate the gardener who came
to open it told him that the signorina was at
vespers.

Giovanni dismissed the carriage and walked
down towards the church. The sun had set but
the sky was clear with the soft calm light of a
spring evening. The country was freshly green
with the tender youth of April and the air was

soft and fragrant. And yet Giovanni felt himself
in some way foreign to this silent spot, with all
the doors closed as if it were the abode of the
dead. He told himself again and again that it was
an hour when every soul was at church, and that
before and after the service those houses were in-
habited and the streets alive with people. As he
got near the church he heard the shrill notes of
the singers: " *Tantum Ergo.*" They would ere
long be coming out, and he walked up and down
waiting. It was certainly strange to see this
fashionable apparition lingering in the rustic village sanctuary. Everything about him betrayed
long habits of wealth and luxury; in his haste to
be off he had not thought of getting himself up in
a travelling-suit, and his town costume, black,
shining, and tightly fitting, with polished shoes,
colored silk socks, and a pair of kid gloves, were
out of keeping in this sylvan scene. The church
was crowded and the doors were ajar; a good
many worshippers who had not come in time to
find room within were kneeling on the grass outside. No sooner had the women caught sight of
this handsome visitor than they began to nudge
each other with their elbows, to giggle, to stare at

him over their shoulders; then, whispering and smiling, they entirely forgot to sing. The men meanwhile, noticing all these manœuvres looked round open-mouthed in the midst of a long-drawn note, and fixed their gaze on the stranger, pouring out their petitions in his direction as though he were the Almighty of whom they were imploring a good harvest, in his own language, the Latin of which they did not understand a word. Then there was a silence. The voice of the priest was heard within uttering the *Oremus;* they all bowed their heads in speechless prayer. A faint scent and a dense mist of incense were diffused and then, after another pause of profound stillness, the baritone chant was heard again without any organ or choir: " The Lord be praised !" and all responded: " The Lord be praised !"

For a few minutes after the harsh mechanical patter of voices in common supplication was to be heard like the croaking of a flock of crows. Then the peasants came slowly and sleepily out, all talking of the fine gentleman from Novara who had arrived during the service and had not knelt down nor even crossed himself:

" It was a perfect Gomorrah was that place, a

den of corruption and a disgrace to the country !
It was not for nothing that never a year passed
without storms or dearth, and that the harvests
were so bad and the grapes failed. The land-
owners had no religion left, and the Lord was fain
to punish them, and then the poor peasants had
nothing to eat; the righteous must suffer for the
sins of the wicked. . ."

The women did not look so far into a mill-
stone; they were more frivolous in their comments.

"Did you see how shiny his shoes were? and
his socks were made of silk! His handkerchief is
worked like a lady's, and as he went by me it
smelt quite sweet," and they giggled in a shame-
faced way. The children did not trouble themselves with so many reflections; they stood round
him in a circle, with their noses in the air, and
their hands behind their backs, as if he had come
there for their express and sole amusement. The
little crowd grew every instant and the new-comers
pushed and elbowed to get front places, and when
the first arrivals elbowed back again and insisted
on their rights: "Make room for me; do you want
to keep the sight all to yourself?"

The last to come out were the ladies, the wives of the village dignitaries; the apothecary's wife, a little dark woman who had always been curiously deficient in hair and teeth, and was so much the color of parchment that time had been unable to do her any great damage; the secretary's wife, who could no longer be called fair, whether hapless or no, because she was quite grey; but who walked as upright as ever, with her head erect and her pinched features, as she talked to some young girls in the most sentimental manner—two girls who had grown and altered too much for Giovanni to know who they were.

Last of all came Rachel. She wore a black silk dress and a black lace shawl over her head. Her brilliant complexion had become rather too highly colored; her figure, which was tall and well made, had lost its grace and slenderness; her hair, which was still fair and yellow, was smoothly drawn back from her temples and twisted into a knot behind; a plait round her head came low on her forehead, framing in her face after the fashion of some of Raphael's Madonnas. But this, like them, was antique in style. She was not dressed like the majority of provincial fine ladies, in the

fashion of the past year, nor yet in the very latest
fashion copied from a colored fashion plate with
original additions and exaggerations. Her dress
consisted simply of a tight bodice and a skirt with
no flounces or trimmings; and her shawl, which
was of fine Chantilly lace, was thrown over her
head and shoulders and knotted in front in the
fashion of the costume worn by Genoese women.
This attire, which made no pretentions to elegance
and was in fact quite devoid of it, was not in the
least ridiculous; its utter simplicity did not attract
attention, and in this rural place it was more appropriate than town-made frills and furbelows.
But it made her look old.

A vision passed before Giovanni's eyes of the
figure that this matronly maiden would make
dressed like a rich lady in the midst of the flutter-
ing brilliant and gracious women of Milan society;
it struck him that she would be nothing less than
ridiculous and he examined her with a feeling of
dissatisfaction. At this moment Rachel turned
her eyes upon him — those large calm eyes and
her placid face, and the shade of contempt in his
expression did not escape her. She recognized
him instantly; but she too gained a painful im-

pression from his youthful figure and his air of fashion and expenditure; she felt that they were parted by a wide gulf. She colored to the roots of her hair, turned her head, and went on her way without glancing at him again, as if she had not known him.

Living in such complete isolation, she had not learnt to hide her feelings under the assumption of gay cordiality, or smile and bow to the man whose mere presence had set her heart throbbing; to offer him her hand with cool ease and talk to him of anything and everything except their relations to each other. Her first impulse on seeing Giovanni was to fly to meet him with her arms outspread, and shed on his breast that torrent of tears which in her joy and surprise had welled up to her throat and was choking her. But her natural shyness, which years of solitude had increased, paralyzed her.

All these emotions had rushed over her in an instant as she saw and recognized Giovanni; but in the next she felt the shock of disappointment that the sight of her had produced in him and she fell from the height of bliss to the depths of mortified discomfiture.

Giovanni followed her with a fixed gaze ; she walked slowly, with a firm and measured step; she was tall and large, and there was something heavy and matronly in her gait as well as in her appearance. As a figure in this grand landscape of plain and mountain this dignified simplicity and shy stateliness were suitable and harmonious ; a painter might have taken this Rachel as a model for the daughter of Laban, or a sculptor have idealized her for a Juno. Giovanni, too, could admire her, but as he would have admired some peasant matron. The idea he had formed of his future wife was something quite different.

His immediate impulse was to rush back to Borgomanero and take the next train to Milan without ever going to see Rachel — to fly in short.

But his heart was soft towards her. He remembered the fair young girl whom he had left twelve years since with a bright future before her; with youth, grace and intelligence, all that might have made her one of the most attractive women of her age. She was rich ; she might have married to live in a capital and lead a brilliant life ; and instead of this she had shut herself up in her old castle, had spent the best years of her life in loneliness, letting the natural spirits of her youth evaporate, neglecting the charms of her person, and yielding dully to the grave and sober influences that time had shed over her, loyally renouncing every ambition, every art that might render her attractive since she had no care to attract those who were within her ken, and the only man whom she would have cared to please was far away. All this she had done for him.

He recalled the evening by the terrace wall when he had asked her: "Will you be mine?" And the blushing girl had replied in words of love; and he, scratching his hands and tearing his clothes, had dragged himself up to reach her foot and kissed his hand for having touched it. Since that day what privations and sufferings he had known! He had toiled for years and they both had endured long waiting for the moment that had at last arrived. And now, when it was present, he would have willingly given all the fame and wealth he had so laboriously acquired to feel for one instant the perfect joy he had then known in touching and kissing that foot!

But it was dead — dead for ever. Time had

killed it. The mere sight of Rachel had sufficed
to convince him that the habit of years had trans-
formed her into a country dame. She was still
Rachel but she was no longer his ideal; and his
heart beat no faster as he saw her once more.

CHAPTER XXXII.

GIOVANNI walked round the church-yard to
give the people time to disperse; but the children
pursued him, clattering on the stones with their
wooden shoes. He took refuge in a path that ran
along the bank of the river and beneath a wall, so
narrow that there was only room for one person
at a time; and the little rustics, less persevering
than the natives of suburban villages, seeing that
the gentleman wanted to be rid of them, stood a
few minutes to stare after him and then dispersed.

Giovanni knew this spot, and he wandered up
and down for some time on the bank where he
had so often loitered in order not to be disturbed
in his day-dreams. At last he slowly made his
way up to the castle. He could no longer picture

to himself the conservatory boudoir, the rocking-chairs, the artistic trifles and the elegant and fragrant nest in which he had dreamed of seeing the fair recluse of his imaginings.   He was depressed and saddened.   The dusk was deepening into darkness; the hills and plain were sinking into monochrome and from the meadows rose a thin mist which looked like a lake.   The natives had gone indoors to supper; the cicala was silent; now and again a cricket chirped and broke the solemn silence.

Giovanni looked up at the castle and saw Rachel standing outside the gate-way leaning over the bridge and gazing down into the moat.   "She is waiting for me," he thought.

But Rachel was in fact so lost in thought that she had not perceived him.   It was not till he was at quite a short distance that she became aware of his approach, and then, instead of going forward to meet him, she went hastily in, as if to fly from him.   This excess of bashfulness utterly disconcerted the town-bred lawyer.   The blush that had dyed her face when she had recognized him in the church-yard, and her lingering to meditate on the bridge proved that his presence had stirred her deeply; and yet she avoided him with sheepish timidity. He shook his head in uneasy doubt and sighed as he entered the gate.

In the court-yard he met a maid who showed him into the great drawing-room. This room, which had impressed him so strongly on the occasion of his last visit to Signor Pedrotti, now struck him as nothing less than grotesque. The heavy stuffed chairs were out of date without being venerable, and their old-fashioned but modern make, with padded backs, was out of keeping with the mediæval mouldings and doorways. Over the old chimney-piece towered a huge bronze clock, picked out with gold, and flanked by monumental candelabra, all three dutifully covered from the dust by glass shades. By the side of the old-fashioned grand pianoforte, music, no less antiquated, was neatly arranged on a shelf. There were no elegant trifles, no books, no flowers, no plants, no newspapers, no photographs, nor engravings, nor any of the pretty and tasteful things that a cultivated woman likes to have about her. Instead of the aromatic scent of burning pine-cones, or the perfume of fresh violets, there was the stuffy smell of a room that is but rarely

used.   It was the unaired and neglected drawing-
room of a house where no company ever comes.
The solitude in which Rachel lived was not
that of Giovanni's cultivated acquaintance, broken
now and again by the intrusion of some choice
spirits—a tea-drinking with a small and privileged
circle, who could keep up the habit of social inter-
course and the vigor of wit and sense, with that
grain of womanly vanity which lends salt and
savor to a gifted nature.   This was real solitude,
oblivion, utter detachment from the world in which
he lived and which had become to him an element
as indispensable as the air he breathed.

Rachel came in, blushing deeply and with an
embarrassed manner.   She only said:

"Oh! Signor Giovanni; how are you?" and
then she seated herself on a sofa.

For an instant Giovanni himself had a spasm
of awkwardness in the presence of this shy and
wordless woman. But still, without exactly knowing why, this cold reception set him more at his
ease than a warmer demonstration would have
done. He took courage, and offering her his hand,
in which she put hers for a moment but hastily
withdrew it, he said:

"I have been long in coming, Rachel." She
colored more deeply than ever. Then he had
come for her? He remembered his promise? It
was not all at an end? She could hardly believe
it! After all these years, in which she had accustomed herself to feel that she was forgotten, and
to believe that she should never marry . . . The
happy surprise gripped so suddenly at her heart
that she almost lost her breath and she could
make no reply. Giovanni, puzzled by her silence,
went on :

"You do not reproach me for my long
delay ?"

"Better late than never," said Rachel, for the
sake of saying something, though the sense of
the proverb as applied to herself did not strike
her.

Her brain and heart were too full of new and
vital impressions that had come on her like a
whirlwind. "Then that dream of her youth was
not dead ; she had fancied that she was too old
for love, and she found that love was still within
her reach ; it was a sort of resurrection !—But was
it possible that this handsome man with his cold
proud face was the Giovanni of old ? and felt as he

had then? No. Then he would have been agitated
at meeting her, his eyes would have looked into
hers and filled with tears, or have flashed with the
lightning of passion. The eyes that met hers now
were not those of a lover; that cool, easy manner,
those tranquil tones, that keen, searching gaze
which examined her as though counting the hairs
on her head and seeking for a wrinkle in her
brow, had no alliance with love. This handsome
city gentleman did not love her!—But why then
had he come?"

Why? He himself supplied the answer to the
question she had uttered.

"Very true; better late than never," he repeated. And then, after a pause—a short pause
during which Rachel had made her rapid reflections, he went on: "Then you do not think that
it is too late?"

Too late! This then was the explanation of
his coldness. He had felt it to be his duty to return
to her, but having returned, having met her again,
he had seen and felt that twelve years had passed
over the girl he remembered. Twelve years of
seclusion, spent among boors, and in rustic occu-
pations; and those twelve years had aged her and

left her unpolished, they had destroyed the ideal
being of whom he had dreamed — a graceful and
cultivated being — and turned her into an honest
country land-owner.   Yes, it was too late!   She
had lost her youth and charm, but she had kept
good sense enough to make her aware of it.

" It is true," thought she.   " I am too old for
love-making, and I am too provincial for him ; he
is ready to marry me but only out of a sense of
loyalty."

An acute and crushing pain clutched at her
heart.   The suspicion that she had felt when they
first met that she had made an unfavorable impression on him became a certainty.   Her soul
died within her as she sat there, bolt upright and
motionless on the sofa, with her hands folded in
her lap, and her eyes fixed on her hands.

Giovanni felt that he must speak again; but
he did not know what to say.   He had come with
the express purpose of asking Rachel to marry
him and now he was afraid of committing himself.
However, there was no escape ; their present relations as much as their old pledge made it inevitable.   He must speak, cost what it might, and
trust to fate.

" Better late than never," he said again. " We still have time to keep our old promises. . ."

" Good Heavens, no !" cried she, choking with tears at his calmness which mortified her bitterly. " Do not let us speak of the past !"

" Why not ?" asked Giovanni, in the soothing tone which we use when we feel that we have much to forgive.

" Because it is too late to think of — some things. . ."

He looked regretfully at her and replied politely :

" Nay, how can you think so ? You are still young. . ." But his eyes were on her as he spoke with a compassionate expression as much as to say :

" But you are right ; it is a pity. . ."

" No," she repeated, " we have followed different roads. . ." She began firmly, but as she spoke her eyes filled with tears and her voice broke. If she had said a word more of what she meant to say : " Our promises were childish folly," she must have burst into weeping, for the mere thought of saying anything so stern had swelled

17

her breast with a sob and she was obliged to be silent to check it. ˙

Giovanni, seeing her so much disturbed, rose to go, saying:

"You will think better of it, Rachel. I have taken you by surprise. I will come back when you are calmer. . ."

Of course — he would come back; he could not cut the matter short in this way.

In all Fontanetto there was not an inn where a gentleman of any pretensions could spend a night. There was nothing left for it but to return to Borgomanero on foot.

"I will stay there a day or two," he said, "so as to give you time. . ."

It was a long walk; a straight road gleaming white in the broad cold moonlight. During this walk of more than an hour he thought over all they had said to each other. Yes, it was too true; those twelve years had done the work of twenty on Rachel. There was not a trace left of the slight, fresh-tinted graceful girl of the past. It would not be flattering to his vanity to introduce this mature bride to the fashionable world of Milan; he would be laughed at — they would say that he had married for money — for Rachel was rich.

So long as he had dreamed of that fair young girl he had never thought of the possible comments of the gossips on her wealth ; but now he wanted to excuse himself for his own recalcitrancy. He reflected, to be sure, that those twelve years had passed over his head also, but then every one knows that a man does not age as a woman does; and he knew many a man of six and thirty who had married girls of eighteen or twenty and who were not thought ridiculous.

But it was not age alone that he cared about; he was superior to such trifling considerations. He considered rather the position he held in the world; he was a distinguished man, about to be elected deputy to parliament; what he wanted was a wife who knew the ways of the world, used to town life, who could receive and make a figure in society, and do him credit in his own house. . .

Rachel, as he had found her, rustic, shy, old-fashioned, could not fill the place. She had herself acknowledged it and shown her good sense. It would be indelicate in him to reopen the argument and renew a scene which had evidently been painful to her. "Her woman's pride had been hurt, for it must always touch a woman's vanity to realize her age and the ravages of time on her charms."

It was a sad — a very sad thing that his ideal should thus have vanished out of his life. He thought of it all night; he thought of it next day in the railway carriage, when, all things considered, he had made up his mind to return to Milan without seeing Rachel again. He thought of it again when he got to Milan — often and always. But always of that ideal as he had remembered it and worshipped it so many years ago — young, sweet, and lovely . . . Perhaps he may yet meet with it in real life, for the mature mistress of the castle of Fontanetto is no longer that ideal.

And Rachel? She no sooner was left alone than she flung herself down, hiding her face on the faded pillows of the old sofa, and broke into a long and desperate fit of weeping.

She knew at once that Giovanni would not come back.

THE END.